LUCIE BABBIDGE'S
HOUSE

LUCIE BABBIDGE'S HOUSE

Sylvia Cassedy

THOMAS Y. CROWELL   NEW YORK

Library of Congress Cataloging-in-Publication Data
Cassedy, Sylvia.
    Lucie Babbidge's house / Sylvia Cassedy.
        p.   cm.
    Summary: Having found a dollhouse full of dolls in the orphanage
where she leads an unhappy existence, Lucie creates a secret life for herself.
    ISBN 0-690-04796-7 : $ — ISBN 0-690-04798-3 (lib. bdg.) :
$
    [1. Dolls—Fiction.   2. Orphans—Fiction.   3. Emotional problems—
Fiction.]   I. Title.
PZ7.C26851Lu 1989   89-1296
[Fic]—dc19   CIP
                                                                        AC

1   2   3   4   5   6   7   8   9   10
First Edition

For Meg and Eva

CONTENTS

LUCIE BABBIDGE'S
HOUSE

PART ONE

CHAPTER ONE

Beans

Miss Pimm handed out the beans, one to each girl. Lucie's bean was hard and smooth, like an ivory bead, and it bulged into a head, all fat and round, at one end. The beans were magic, Miss Pimm told them, and someone at the rear of the room gasped: "Ooh!" It was Emily. "Magic!"

"How are they magic, class?" Miss Pimm asked, ignoring Emily, or not hearing. "Lucie?" she called, although Lucie's hand had not gone up.

"I don't know, Miss Pimm," Lucie answered, not raising her head. She was busy rubbing the ivory surface of her bean with a thumb, liking its feel. What was it that felt like that? The round brass knob on the door to her house? The crown of the alabaster king in her chess set? The dome of her piano teacher's smooth, shiny head? All of these.

"Lucie?" Miss Pimm didn't always hear when Lucie spoke.

"I don't know, Miss Pimm," she said again, though no louder than before, and still not lifting her head.

"I don't know, Miss Pimm." This time the voice was nice and loud, but it wasn't Lucie's; it was Rose Beth's. Rose Beth was doing her imitation of Lucie, and as usual it was wrong. Lucie never spoke in that high baby whine, and she didn't wag her head back and forth like that, either. Her voice, when she spoke—if she spoke at all—was a soft kind of whisper, hoarse and fuzzy: what Miss Pimm called a croak. And she kept her head quite still, with her chin settled firmly in the hollow of her throat. But Rose Beth wasn't trying to be accurate; she was trying to make everybody laugh. Which everybody did. Even so, she got the legs part right. Lucie always sat like that, with her heels apart and her knees together. "Like a camel," Anna once said. "No, a goose." That was Claire. "Which is what she is. Goosey-Loosey."

"How are the beans magic, class?" Miss Pimm repeated.

Emily's hand went up. "If you plant them, a beanstalk will grow? With a house on top and a giant?" But that was not how. This was botany class, not reading. The beans were magic because they contained the secret of life, Miss Pimm finally told them. They were magic because they could be transformed.

"*Transformed!*" she exclaimed. "Transformed into living, growing miracles, ten, a hundred, a *thousand* times their present size." In a few weeks, she continued, green vines would spread up the windows and along the cords that raised and lowered the shades. "Next month, in this very room, a jungle will exist where no jungle existed before."

"A jungle?" Charlotte asked.

Lucie pressed her bean into the palm of her hand, and with the point of a marking pen drew on its bulging head a little red face: an eye, an eye, a mouth—dot, dot, circle.

"A veritable jungle," Miss Pimm recited, as though this really *was* a reading class, not a lesson on plants, and she was delivering the lines of a poem. "Thick as a curtain of the stoutest green cloth," she finished.

"Look what she's doing," Charlotte whispered, or half whispered; the words were plain to Lucie, five seats away.

"Who?" Daisy was working a puzzle in her lap.

"Goosey-Loosey."

"Ugh, her." It was a number puzzle, and Lucie could hear the little squares slide along their tracks. "What's she doing now?"

Lucie had tried a puzzle like that once herself, long ago, but the 13 and the 14 and the 15 had come out wrong all the time. Still, it had been nice, pushing all those numbers up and down, back and forth. She'd pretended they were children in a classroom, and they'd been asked to rank themselves, smart to dumb, in proper rows. Only the three at the bottom, so dumb they couldn't even find their own seats, were out of place.

"She's messing up her bean," Charlotte half whispered some more. "She's smearing it all over with red."

"With blood, probably," Daisy said.

"A thick, green jungle," Miss Pimm went on, "and it will spring from the beans that you hold in your hands. Can anyone think of a magic more wonderful than that?"

No one could.

"She messes up everything," Daisy added. "She messes up *herself*. Look at her. With her hair in those knots and all."

"And that juice down her front."

"Each bean is a seed," Miss Pimm continued, "and in the blink of an eye the magic will take place. But first we must provide the seeds with the environment they need. Who can tell us what a growing plant's environment must be?"

"Dirt and water?" Emily asked, and this time she was right, although she'd forgotten to mention light, and you weren't supposed to say "dirt" in science class. You were supposed to say "a fertile planting medium." Miss Pimm wrote the words on the board.

They were all handed little paper cups after that— "seed starters," Miss Pimm called them—and she walked up and down the rows with a bag of loose, dry soil. "Leave a good half inch at the top," she cautioned, as the girls poured small mounds into their cups. Lucie dug out a scoopful when it came her turn, and then another and another until the cup toppled over and the soil ran out on her desk.

"*Mind!*" Miss Pimm cried out. "Mind what you *do!*" and she jumped quickly back, as though something scalding had been spilled.

"Slob," Daisy whispered.

"Crazy," Charlotte whispered back.

"Crazy slob." And Claire, from across the row, whispered her favorite word, which was "swine."

"What did Lucie fail to do?" Miss Pimm liked to ask the class questions about Lucie. "What did Lucie forget to wear today?" she would sometimes begin, or "What did Lucie do to her face?" as though Lucie were a demonstration on a table.

"Follow directions, Miss Pimm," Anna replied. Everyone had to say "Miss Pimm this" and "Miss Pimm that." Norwood Hall was that kind of school.

"What directions?" Miss Pimm persisted.

"Leave a good half inch at the top?" Claire said, making it a question, although of course she knew she was right.

"Lucie, you have made a disgusting mess. Disgusting." Miss Pimm always divided that word in two.

"Dizz gusting," she would say, and her face would sour. "Sweep it from your desk," she ordered now, moving on to the next row.

Lucie made a little curved wall with her hand and guided all the dirt onto her skirt. It made a pleasant hill, like a sandpie, in her lap, and she stirred it once or twice with a thumb.

Once, long ago, she had built another sandpie—a real one that time, with real sand, at the border of the sea. What sea? Where? Someone kneeling near her had shown her how. Someone in a hat of creamy straw had whisked a shovel back and forth, and there—like sudden magic—stood a tower, flat and stiff, the shape, the *perfect shape*, of the air inside her pail. "Oh, Lucie," she had said, that someone in a hat, "it looks good enough to eat," and suddenly, amazingly, she *did* eat it, or pretend to, taking little nibbles from the shovel.

It had been her mother, that was who, although try as Lucie might she could conjure up no features on the face beneath that hat.

"Lucie!" Miss Pimm cried. "Stop that! Class! What has Lucie done?"

"Made a dizz gusting mess, Miss Pimm," Emily said. It was her second correct answer that day.

"It's a custard pie, Lucie," said her mother that day, crouching knee to knee beside her at the sea. "I can tell by the way it cools my tongue."

"Lucie, we plant seeds in a cup, not in our laps."
Miss Pimm liked to speak that way to Lucie, telling
her what everybody knew—what Lucie herself knew—
very well. "Food goes in the *mouth*, Lucie," she would
sometimes say, "not on one's blouse." Or, "A pencil is
a writing tool, Lucie, not an instrument for cleaning
one's ear." Then she would add, "I never. I never saw
the *like*." Her upper teeth would catch on her lip when
she said the "v" in "never," and her eyes would grow
wide, so wide that white showed all around. Rose Beth
sometimes copied her after class.

"Yes, Miss Pimm," Lucie said now, and pinch by
pinch she transferred the little mound from her skirt
to the cup, holding her fingers just high enough to
make a nice shower.

"Stop playing with the *dirt!*" Miss Pimm shouted, and
Claire whispered, "Swine."

Pushing hard with their thumbs, the girls buried their
beans in the soft black dirt—it *was* dirt, after all; Miss
Pimm had just said so—until no trace could be seen.
Then, from a pitcher that was passed up and down,
they floated a puddle of water on each smooth, flat
top.

They wrote their names in marking pen on their
cups after that, and carried them to the windowsill.
Claire used a different color for each letter of her name,

9

and Rose Beth and Emily added flowered decorations as well, but Miss Pimm reminded them that this was botany, not art.

"And what is botany?" she asked. Claire raised her hand, but Miss Pimm chose to answer her question herself. "The study of botany," she told everyone, "is the study of miracles. Miracles in the world of plants. We will witness two miracles, class, when we plant our beans. Who will remind us of the first miracle of the beans? Jane?"

"There's going to be a jungle in here, Miss Pimm."

"The beans will sprout and produce vines in great profusion. The second miracle will occur many weeks later," Miss Pimm told them, but she didn't say what it would be. It was to be a surprise.

Lucie's marking pen had dried up halfway through writing her name, and her cup displayed the letters "LUC."

"Hey, Goosey-Loosey, it says Luc!" Anna pulled the cup from Lucie's hand. "Like *bad* luck, get it? Hey, Daisy, look. Goose's cup is bad luck."

"Ooh, make it say that on her cup. Write bad luck, in purple."

"No, green. Green for poison."

"Hey, yeah. Something poison's going to grow from Goose's bean."

"Poison ivy is what. Look, Enid. Poison ivy's going to grow in Goose's cup."

"Ooh, get it away."

"No, get *her* away. Poison ivy's catching."

"Push her over to the wall."

"No, don't touch her. You'll get blisters. Use this stick. Poke her in the back with it."

"Yeah, like she's a marshmallow."

"Let's roast her."

"Yeah, let's have roast Goose."

"Move, Goose. *Move.*"

"Move."

"MOVE!"

"Move some more, Goosey-Loosey."

"No, *more.*"

"Hey, look what happened. The stick broke."

"Then we'll each take a piece. One for me, one for you. There she *goes!*"

"*Move,* Goose, MOVE!"

"I can't," Lucie answered, speaking at last. "I'm already here," she said into the wall, in that hoarse fuzzy whisper that Miss Pimm called a croak.

CHAPTER TWO

The Secret

"Olive!" Lucie called as she opened the front door of her house. "Olive, Olive, Olive!" There was no need, really, to call out. Olive was right there in the front hall, with the small white apron tied around her waist as always, and the frilled cap stuck on her head. But, "Olive," Lucie said again, because Olive was a name she liked to say. Once, long ago, she had *eaten* an olive, the fruit kind, and she never had forgotten what it was like. Its flavor had been a shock and one that couldn't be described—bitter? salty? sour? it was none of these—but its feel was what she remembered best of all: round and smooth and wonderful in her mouth. And that was how Olive's name felt when she spoke it: like a marble rolling green on her tongue. *Olive.*

"Where is Emmett?" Lucie asked.

"Getting up from his nap," Olive answered. She leaned against the stove, but then remembered it was hot.

"No, I'm not," Emmett said. "I'm coming down from it," and there he was in the hallway, his pants all rumpled from sliding down the stairs and his shirt untucked at the waist.

And there was Mumma, too, happy to see Lucie and not rumpled at all, but very tidy, with her face all pink and smooth, except for a few lines, and her dress smooth, too; smooth as satin. It *was* satin, which was why.

"Oh, Lucie," Mumma said, "you're so pretty in that dress. Hold still for a moment and let me see just how pretty you are. Do you know, if I were an artist, I would paint you right away, just as you look in the doorway, with that dress I always liked and the flower in your hair."

"Paint her!" Emmett exclaimed. "What's the matter with the color she already is?"

"Stop that, Emmett," Olive said. "You know very well what your mother means." And that was true. He did.

"Come, Lucie." Mumma laid her hand on Lucie's shoulder and led her into the drawing room, while Emmett slid along two steps behind. "Come and tell us what you learned in school today." Mumma's hand perched like a familiar bird alongside Lucie's ear, and traveled with her as they crossed the room.

"Oh, I learned lots of lovely things," Lucie said. She sat alongside her mother before a table set with little cups and plates. Emmett lay on the rug with his nose to the ceiling, and Olive waited in the doorway to be told what to bring.

"Like what, Lucie?" Mumma asked. "Olive, we'll have those little ginger cookies today."

"Like how to make a sandpie in my lap."

"A sandpie in your lap! Oh, Lucie, remember the sandpies we used to make beside the sea?" And she drew closer to Lucie and to the memory hanging between them, so that they could listen to it together, ear to ear. "Remember how I nibbled at the shovel?"

Olive came in once more, this time with a tea tray balanced carefully across her wrists.

"'What else?" Emmett asked. He watched as Olive arranged some tea things and a plate of round brown cookies on the table. "What else did you learn in school?"

"I learned how to plant a jungle with a bean, and I decorated a flowerpot, Mumma, with my name all in green."

"It will be a beautiful jungle, Lucie, and the flowerpot will be beautiful, too. Everything you do is beautiful." She walked to the mantel where one of Lucie's drawings hung—a bowl of tiny flowers with petals thin as thread. "Just beautiful."

"I want to go to school, too," Emmett said to the ceiling, "and plant a jungle bean."

"You will, Emmett," Mumma told him. "When you've grown some more."

"How much more?"

"At least another foot."

"Grow another foot!" Emmett raised his heels above his head and examined them. "But Mumma, two are all I need."

"Emmett!" Mumma said, beginning to lose patience, "I mean grow until you reach my elbow."

"But what if you grow, too?"

"I don't grow, Emmett. You know that." But as far as Emmett could tell, he didn't either, and he said he didn't think he'd ever go to school at all. "I'll never get to grow a jungle bean," he said.

Mumma was about to answer, but just then there was a clicking sound from somewhere outside. "Dada!" Emmett cried and Lucie counted the footsteps aloud as they fell: ". . . thirteen, fourteen, fifteen." It always took Dada fifteen steps to round the corner of the house and reach the front door. "Well!" he shouted from the hallway. "Well, well, well," and there he was among them, his newspaper firmly fastened to his arm, his hat firmly fastened to his head. "Well, well, *well!* How nice you all look. Lucie, is that a flower growing from your head?"

He asked that every day. "Let me sprinkle it with

kisses to make it grow." He said *that* every day, too, and then, bending from the waist, he pressed a circle of kisses around the poppy in her hair.

"Sprinkle *me*, too," Emmett said after that, "so I can grow and go to school." Then Dada put little kisses on Emmett's head, and lifted him by the waist to make him tall.

And then, suddenly, Mumma had an announcement to make. "Dada," she said. "Lucie, Emmett. I have a secret to tell."

"A secret!" Emmett cried. "I love secrets, especially when they're about somebody else. Is it about somebody else, Mumma, and is it mean? Is it a mean secret? That's the best kind."

"Tell it to us, Mumma," Lucie said, giving her brother a small push with her toe.

"Oh, Lucie," Emmett said. "She can't *tell* it. If she did, it wouldn't be a secret anymore," and he sat straight up.

"Yes, it would," Lucie answered, "if we kept it from somebody else."

"But I don't know anybody else to keep it *from*," he insisted, and he was right. Emmett had no friends.

"I do," Lucie said. "I know lots of people. You can have some of them. You can have Rose Beth to keep your secret from. And Claire. Now tell it to us, Mumma."

Very slowly, Olive moved across the kitchen floor, into the dining room, across the front hall, and into the drawing room doorway, just as Mumma was saying, "Well, dears, the secret is that we are going to have a new baby."

"A new one!" Emmett cried. "Do some people have old ones?"

"A new baby!" Lucie exclaimed. "When, Mumma? When will it come?"

"After a while. That's when babies always come."

"Boy or girl?" Emmett demanded.

"We don't know, Emmett," Mumma said. "It will be a surprise."

"It can't be much of a surprise, if there are only two things it can be."

"Everything is always a surprise, Emmett, even when there are only two things," Dada told him, "because they always turn out to be the opposite of what you think."

"Well, then," Emmett said, "I shall think the opposite to begin with."

"I never," Olive said, sounding, as she very often did, like Miss Pimm. "I never heard the like," but she meant about the baby, not the surprise.

CHAPTER THREE

Lucie's Letter

"Lucie!" Miss Pimm raised her head from a list in her hand. "Who is Delia Hornsby?"

"I don't know, Miss Pimm." The clock on the school-room wall gave out a hum—a long golden hum that trailed like a wire from the wall to Lucie's ear. *Mmmmmmm*, it went. Which came first, she wondered, the letter "M" or the sound it made? Did a caveman hear a hum once, like the tone of the clock, and decide to call it "M," or was it the other way around? Did he first draw an "M" and then invent a sound to match it?

"You don't know, Lucie? When you yourself wrote her name on the list?"

Rose Beth laughed first, as always. Rose Beth knew, before anyone else, just when Miss Pimm expected them to laugh. Miss Pimm didn't even have to look at her, although sometimes she did anyway. Jane laughed next; the others right after.

"Lucie?"

"The list, Miss Pimm?" A nice piece of skin had loosened on her knuckle, and if she took great care, she might pull it all off at once, in a long, slender strip.

"Pick your head up, Lucie. I am standing by my desk, not in your lap. Look at me when I speak to you."

"Yes, Miss Pimm."

Her skin had flamed with sunburn on that seaside afternoon long ago, and a day or two later little blisters, pale and moist, bloomed like baby mushrooms on her shoulders and her back. Later still, the blisters broke, leaving little shreds of tissue, like the one that clung right now to her knuckle. Her mother had warned her that the blisters would appear. "Oh, Lucie," she had said, that afternoon on the sand, "you'll be a plum. A little boiled plum that I must peel." In the end, though, it was Lucie herself who peeled her skin, lifting off the tatters piece by piece, leaving patches faintly yellow, like the flesh of a plum.

"We're all waiting to hear who Delia Hornsby is," Miss Pimm said now. Her voice took on the tone that she often used with Lucie, when she pretended to be patient but was not.

"She used to own my house, Miss Pimm."

The little shred of knuckle skin lay now on her desk, and she rubbed it into a thin, gray thread.

"She used to what? Speak up, Lucie." It was never clear whether Miss Pimm really didn't hear Lucie or simply pretended not to.

"She was a houseowner, Miss Pimm."

"I see. And does that make her a person of renown?" The laughter was louder this time, but it wouldn't be as loud after the next dumb thing she said. It never was, Lucie knew, the third time around. "Does that make her worthy of a letter?"

Lucie slipped the thread of skin into her mouth and pressed it hard between her teeth. "I don't know, Miss Pimm."

All the other girls had written their letters to what Miss Pimm called personages. "What is a personage?" she had asked, writing the word on the board. "How old someone is," Emily had said, but she was wrong. "Is it like a parsonage," Claire had asked, "except a person lives there instead?" But that was wrong, too. A personage was someone of renown, Miss Pimm told them, although there were those who didn't know what renown was either and both Rose Beth and Daisy had written their letters to movie stars.

Delia Hornsby was not a personage. Lucie herself had never heard of her until she discovered her name scratched into the paint on the back of her house, just below the sill on the dining-room wall. *Delia Hornsby*, it said, and there was an address that was not Lucie's address or one that she had ever heard of. It was in England, and not only that: Delia Hornsby was dead. *1885*, it said in the same tidy hand, right under the

England part, so not only was Delia Hornsby not a personage, she was not even a person, and that was why, when the letter list came around the room, Lucie had written the name Delia Hornsby beside her own. So she wouldn't get a reply. It was a stupid assignment, writing letters to personages.

The strip of skin softened between her teeth, but did not melt. She chewed on it as though it were a rubber band. "She was an interior designer, Miss Pimm. Is, I mean."

Surely you could say that about Delia Hornsby? Hadn't she designed the interior of Lucie's house, painting those scrolls above the lintel, stitching up the hems, just so, on the curtains, knotting the fringes on the rug? Who else could have done all that, so long ago? Didn't that make her an interior designer?

"Of renown?" Miss Pimm wanted to know.

"Yes, Miss Pimm," and she took out a sheet of writing paper from her desk.

"The opening portion of your letter is called the 'salutation,' " Miss Pimm had told them. "It is your way of saluting your correspondent. It is a greeting. Use a proper title of respect in your salutation. Mr., Mrs., or Miss."

"Dear . . ." Lucie began now. Dear what? What were you supposed to call a dead person? Miss? Dear

Miss Hornsby? Could you still be Miss if you were dead? Dear Delia? Delia wasn't a title of respect. Dear Dead Personage?

"Dear Delia Hornsby:" she finally wrote. ("Follow your salutation with a colon," Miss Pimm had reminded them. "Use a comma only if you are addressing a friend. Your personage is not in the category of a friend.")

Dear Delia Hornsby, colon. "Skip two spaces and indent," Miss Pimm had instructed them. "You are now ready to compose the 'body' of your letter. The 'body' is the part that bears your message. Your body can be long or it can be short," she had added, making Claire laugh.

If you folded the top corner of the page over just a little bit, and then curled it back, and folded it over again and curled it back again, and did that over and over, then pretty soon the corner would get soft as cloth, and you could stroke it, like a little ear.

"Lucie? Have you begun your letter?"

"Yes, Miss Pimm."

Dear Delia Hornsby:

I thought you would like to know how your house looks now. Well, it looks simply elegant. (Don't use words unless you are certain of their meaning, Miss Pimm had warned them, but Lucie knew what elegant meant. It was Mumma's favorite word.) *It was all a terrible wreck before we moved in, but everything is beautifully fixed up now, especially the drawing room, which looks very elegant.* (Don't repeat words needlessly, Miss Pimm had said.) ... *which looks very grand,"* Lucie wrote instead. (Grand was another of Mumma's favorite words. She even said that people were grand. "Your father is a grand person," she would tell Emmett and Lucie, and Emmett would ask, "Then is he my grandfather?" And after that he would ask, "And do we have a grand piano, too?" but Mumma would say no, it was an upright.) *The kitchen is the only room that isn't quite grand,* Lucie continued. *Olive complains about it all the time. She's our maid. Mostly she complains about the icebox.*

Letters were supposed to be lively, Miss Pimm had reminded them. "Tell about yourselves in a *lively* fashion. Provide interesting details," and she had read them a letter that Louisa May Alcott had once sent to her mother and was all about market women selling snails in France.

If you came to visit now, Lucie's letter went on to say, *you would find some changes, but mostly everything is the same. There's a new leg on the piano, and a lot of things are probably rearranged, but the curtains are the same and so are the rugs. Also the bathroom, which still has that flush thing at the ceiling. Emmett thinks that goblins live up there. He's five.*

I'm eleven. I sleep in the front bedroom, the one with the little alcove, and Emmett sleeps in the room next door to mine. My parents are in the big bedroom in the back, and next to that is

23

the little room that's supposed to be for sewing, but we have nothing to sew, so mostly we use it for hide and seek. Olive sleeps in the attic. And Greenheart sleeps in his cage. He's my bird.

They were also supposed to ask questions about their personage. "Show an interest in your correspondent. Inquire about his career," Miss Pimm had advised them, "or hers. Ask about the nature of his work, and how he prepared for it educationally. Perhaps he can offer some advice on how you may prepare for a career like that yourselves."

What was it like being an interior designer? Lucie finished, and then came the complimentary close part. "The 'complimentary close' is the letter writer's way of saying good-bye. If your letter is a formal one, close it with 'Yours truly' or 'Very truly yours.' In a less formal letter, use 'Sincerely.' " Which was Lucie's? Could a letter be very formal if it said things about the bathroom? Probably not, but Lucie picked "Very truly yours" just the same, even though she couldn't be very truly anybody's who was dead.

> *Very truly yours,*
> *Lucie Babbidge*

Probably she shouldn't have put in the part about the bathroom at all. Miss Pimm would not approve, but then Miss Pimm would never see it. It was a sin to read other people's mail; that was the final thing Miss Pimm had told them about letters. "Letters are sacred," she had told them. "Remember that, girls. It is sinful to invade something sacred. That is an inviolate rule. Who can tell us the meaning of inviolate?"

"Purple?" Anna had suggested.

And Delia herself would never see it, because she was dead. Someday next month or the month after that, the letter would come back, all covered with messages stamped in red: RETURN TO SENDER, they would say, and a red-ink hand in a neat square cuff would point a finger: THIS PERSON IS DEAD, or however those messages read. Lucie would find out soon enough.

"My personage is dead, Miss Pimm," she would explain, but by then it would be too late to pick a new one. The letter-writing project would be over and they would be doing something else. With her tongue, she scraped the shred of skin from her teeth and let it slide down her throat.

CHAPTER FOUR

Lucie's House

Lucie Babbidge's house *was* rather elegant, although not so elegant as she had made out in her letter, and not so big either. Still, it was a fine house, with three stories, if you counted the attic, and more than enough space for the four of them and Olive. Lucie, in fact, had almost two rooms to herself—the big one where the bed was, and the alcove. What had the alcove been used for when the house had belonged to Delia Hornsby? she wondered. A baby, most likely, but the Babbidges' new baby, when it came, would sleep in the sewing room alongside Mumma and Dada's room. The cradle was already set up.

Lucie used the alcove for guests—Emmett, when he agreed to come; Mumma when he did not. The game table, with its chess set, was kept there, and so was the birdcage, with its single green tenant. "Sing, Greenheart," Lucie would say to it each day, and it would answer with three high tweets.

The chess set was quite old and there were only four

men. They weren't even men: The king was an alabaster lion and the bishop an ebony sheep. Lucie made up games with them, dancing the lion across a floor tiled red and black.

The dining room was to the right of the downstairs hallway, the drawing room to the left. Any other family would have called the drawing room the living room, but Mumma liked "drawing room" better. "It's far more elegant," she always said.

"But no one ever draws in it at all," Emmett protested.

"Not that kind of drawing," Lucie told him.

"What kind, then?" but Lucie didn't know.

The piano, the one with the leg that didn't match, stood at one end of the drawing room. The tea table stood at the other, right in front of a sofa that all of them could sit on if they squeezed. All of them, that is, but Olive, who was not expected to sit in the drawing room at all and besides never sat anywhere.

"I would wrinkle my dress," she explained.

The dining room was used for parties mostly, or for playing big games. Every now and then, Dada would announce, "Lucie, Emmett. I feel like a big game today," and Emmett would say, "What kind of big game do you feel like, Dada? Moose or antelope or what?" and Dada would say, "Donkey."

Then all four of them—five, if Olive played too—

would line up, one behind the other, and play donkey, with blindfolds tied around their heads and little paper tails in their hands.

They ate their meals in the kitchen, which was the least elegant room of all, what with the icebox made of wood and the churn that didn't churn.

"It's nothing but a dustbin," Olive always said of the churn, and that's where she thrust Dada's umbrella the day its silk got torn to shreds.

And the stove! "How can you expect me to cook on such a thing!" Olive exclaimed to no one in particular. But cook she did, after a fashion, on a stove made of iron and attached to the wall with a thick, black pipe. "And with only two pots!" There were three, but one had a hole that a pea could slip through, and it stood on the dining-room table, holding flowers.

Emmett's room was not quite so large as Lucie's, but it was pretty large, all the same—large enough for all the members of his Noah's ark to march across the floor every evening so he could feed them their daily meal: make-believe oats from his fingertips and palmfuls of pretend hay.

The attic had a good high ceiling, so no one had to stoop—not even Dada, the tallest of them all—and a window at each end for light to come through. It contained a great number of things collected long ago—by Delia Hornsby, most likely—and stored up there because they didn't fit anywhere else: a chair without a seat beside the window, a wooden chandelier against the wall, and a wardrobe made of oak, or so Mumma said.

"Solid oak," she told them—and Emmett asked if oak was ever liquid—but its door was gone and you could see what lay inside. Olive's things, they were. Clothes mostly, although not a great many. "There's no need," Olive used to say, and she was right. A frill of an apron over her "proper black" did quite well enough, she assured everyone, for the chores around the house; and besides, there were few visitors to entertain. Outside of Lucie and the family, in fact, there were none. (Mr. Broome didn't get entertained until much later.) The clothes in the wardrobe were a pair of satin gloves and a pile of cotton somethings that she called her flannels, but that Lucie knew to be something else. Underwear.

A bathtub was up there, too. A large wooden tub, too large for downstairs, and anyway, it wasn't hooked up to any water. Olive now and then lay inside it, fully dressed. She took dry baths, she explained, "so as not to catch a chill," and she was right in that, too; in all the time she had been with the Babbidges, she hadn't been sick a single day.

CHAPTER FIVE

The Pendletons

"Heads *down!*" Miss Pimm commanded, and they all laid their heads on their desks.

It was after-lunch rest, the only time of the day when doing nothing was the right thing to do. Lucie flattened one cheek against the wood and opened the opposite eye. The long thin scratch below the pencil groove enlarged, elongated, became a river carrying little boats from town to town. Up and down the water the boats slipped, quietly, so no one could hear, and invisibly, too. No one but Lucie knew they were there, and she saw them only once a day, right after lunch. The rest of the time they were invisible to her, too, although they continued on their course, back and forth.

"Lucie, you are not resting."

"Yes, I am, Miss Pimm," she said into the wood. It smelled of something dark.

"No, you are not. You are dangling your arms. Put them under your head. One cannot digest one's food if one's blood must travel to one's hands instead of to one's stomach." Rose Beth's arms were dangling too, but Miss Pimm did not notice and Rose Beth did not move them.

"Yes, Miss Pimm." In ten minutes, rest time would be over, and Miss Pimm would say "Heads *up*!" Then she would reach into her desk drawer and remove from it *The Adventures of the Pendletons,* which was a book about a family that lived in England long ago. Miss Pimm read a chapter aloud every day, right after rest time and just before arithmetic. The Pendletons didn't have any adventures, in spite of the title of the book; nothing very remarkable, in fact, ever happened to them at all. They just *did* things, like everybody else, except that what they did was unlike what most people did now.

Yesterday, Mr. and Mrs. Pendleton and Frank and Josie gathered at the bottom of the garden—that's what they called it: the *bottom* of the garden, as though it were a bowl—and played quoits at the river's edge.

"Who can tell us what 'quoits' is?" Miss Pimm asked, writing the word on the board.

Enid's hand went up. "Some kind of punctuation?" But Enid hadn't been paying attention.

"A game?" Daisy asked.

Of course it was a game, but what *kind?*

"Lucie?"

"I don't know, Miss Pimm," and from across the room, Rose Beth laughed. "She doesn't know any games at all."

"She couldn't play them even if she did," Claire whispered back. "She'd fall on her face."

"She'd fall on her face playing tic-tac-toe," Rose Beth answered, whispering now.

"Charlotte?" Miss Pimm asked. "Can you tell us what quoits is?"

"Is it something like tennis?" But Charlotte was wrong, and so was Anna when she said poker.

"Is it a flattened ring of iron or circle of rope used in a throwing game?" Jane asked, and she was right, because she was reading from a dictionary inside her desk. Lucie could see. Quoits was ringtoss, and Frank missed the wooden rod he was aiming for and threw his ring into the river instead.

" 'Oh, look!' Mrs. Pendleton cried." Miss Pimm pitched her voice high as a bird's when she spoke Mrs. Pendleton's words, and she made them come out British. " 'It's become a little boat.' " Mrs. Pendleton never got angry at anything Frank and Josie did, and neither did Mr. Pendleton. " 'It will sail all the way to America!' " Miss Pimm's voice became very deep as she exclaimed for Mr. Pendleton.

After that, Mr. and Mrs. Pendleton and Frank and Josie made up stories about what would happen when the boat landed in America, and then the sky grew dark and it was time to go inside.

" 'The days are growing shorter,' Mrs. Pendleton announced, 'now that summer is over.'

" 'No, they're not,' Frank objected. 'It still takes twelve hours from breakfast to supper.' Frank was making an error," Miss Pimm told the class. "What was his error? Lucie, can you tell us?"

"No, Miss Pimm."

"She's not listening, Miss Pimm," Jane said.

"Thank you, Jane," Miss Pimm answered, not thanking her at all. Miss Pimm already knew that Lucie wasn't listening. That was why she'd called on her.

"You're welcome, Miss Pimm," Jane replied. "She never listens to the story. She never listens to anything."

But instead of agreeing, Miss Pimm recited her kindness lecture, as she very often did. "Lucie is less fortunate than the rest of us," it always began, as it did now, and it ended with "We must try to be kind." Everybody was always very quiet after the kindness lecture, and they were all especially quiet now, as it had been a long time since the last one.

"Who can tell us what Frank's error was?" Miss Pimm asked again. "Enid?"

"He thought his mother meant the day was short like it didn't last a lot of hours, but she meant it got dark early."

" 'I mean in terms of daylight hours, Frank, dear,' " was how Mrs. Pendleton put it, " 'not in terms of total hours. Winter is approaching and so the sun shines for only a short while every day.'

" 'Every day!' Frank looked alarmed. 'On weekends, too?' Frank's errors are often quite comical," Miss Pimm explained, and then she read about how all the Pendletons walked up the garden path and into the house to have tea at the little table in the drawing room and to play their favorite card game—beggar-my-neighbor.

Today, Josie was sitting at the foot of Mrs. Pendleton's bed, watching her mother prepare for a ball. " 'Oh, wear your rose brocade, Mamma,' " Miss Pimm read, sending her voice into a squeak. " 'M'mah,' " she said. " 'Do wear it. It's my most favorite of all,' " and Mrs. Pendleton said she would, since Josie liked it so very much, and she would carry a paisley shawl, too, as Josie liked that as well and a breeze was coming up. "Who can tell us what paisley is?" Miss Pimm asked.

The lid of Lucie's desk rested on her wrists, and her fingers worked silently in the dark metal bin. The desks in Lucie's classroom were all different. Some were attached to their seats with curved steel pipes that you could slide like a sled across the floor. Some were made of metal, some of wood. Some weren't desks at all: Enid and Jane sat at little square tables, and Charlotte did her work on a fat, flat arm that stretched like something swollen from the side of her chair.

Lucie and Rose Beth each had a desk from long ago, with a round hole in the upper corner that had once held a glass vessel of ink. "An inkwell," Miss Pimm had told them, and Rose Beth had said, "Ugh. A well filled with ink?" Lucie had wondered about that, too: That's what they used to have in her desk? A well of ink? You lowered a bucket and drew up not cold clear water, but some sudden cruel syrup that stained your hands and dripped black all over your shirt?

Whatever it had been, though, it was long since gone, and a circle of light dropped through the open hole into the metal bin below—a nice flat light that made a moon where it fell. Sometimes, with her red marker, Lucie would outline its shape on her notebook, on her spelling words, on the back of her hand. And sometimes, too, with a fist sliding sideways, she could make a slow eclipse, watching as the dark crept from edge to edge until nothing but a sliver—thin as the skin of a grape—was left, and then that would be gone, too.

One, two, three, four, five, Lucie counted to herself now, slipping some paper reinforcements onto the prong of a tack. *One, two, three, four, five,* she counted, slipping them off again. Something stung her thumb—the tiny metal point, sharp as a fang—and she pulled her hand away.

"Lucie's playing with something in her desk, Miss Pimm," Anna said, "when she's supposed to be listening to the story."

A bead of blood rested on Lucie's thumb and she waited for it to dry, so she could pick it off all at once, like a speck of hardened glue. Miss Pimm stopped reading. "Playthings are not allowed in the classroom, Lucie. Bring me what you have, this minute."

"Yes, Miss Pimm." Bring her what? The blood? Lucie looked at the bright-red drop floating like an egg yolk on her finger. "If you freeze a drop of blood it turns to ruby," Daisy once said, and she'd taken Claire and Charlotte into the icy air one noon to show them how. Lucie never learned what had happened after that, but she'd wondered just the same.

"Lucie! Do as you've been asked. Bring me the playthings from your desk."

"Yes, Miss Pimm." She licked her finger clean and swept up the pieces in her desk. The lid banged shut— on the notebook, on the marker, on the flat white moon shining brighter now than ever, in the dark.

Someone—usually it was Anna, but sometimes it was Jane—would always slide a leg across the aisle as Lucie approached, and pull it away again, just in time. But then, someone *else* would put a leg out, and that was the one Lucie would stumble on. Today, though, the first leg—and it was Emily's this time—remained in place, and Lucie caught her ankle on its shin. "Look where you are *going*!" Miss Pimm cried.

"She spilled all her stuff on the floor," Emily told Miss Pimm, although that was plain for everyone to see.

"Pick up what you have dropped and throw it in the trash," Miss Pimm said, and Lucie did, but carefully, one object at a time, so that later she could take it all out again: the little thumbtack she had just that morning pulled from the bulletin board, the five paper reinforcements from Miss Pimm's desk drawer, and the long shred of cloth from the chalk tray.

"We're waiting, Lucie," Miss Pimm said, and they *were* waiting, all of them, for Lucie to straighten up and walk back to her desk so that Miss Pimm could take up the story of the Pendletons and their adventures once again.

Mrs. Pendleton wore satin shoes to the ball and a little silver crown on her head. A tiara. Lucie knew what a tiara was, but she didn't raise her hand when Miss Pimm asked. She never raised her hand.

"*And Mr. Pendleton,*" Miss Pimm read, "*was waiting at the doorway, resplendent in a velvet cutaway coat.*" She didn't have to ask what a cutaway coat was or even explain it because the book had a picture of Mr. Pendleton waiting at the doorway for his wife, and Miss Pimm held it up for everyone to see. Mr. Pendleton did not look resplendent at all, as the drawing was done in black ink. Instead, he looked odd—in pants that were too tight and a coat that had very little front.

"I liked the part about the ball gown best," Charlotte said later.

"Me, too," Emily said, "except Lucie spoiled it all."

"She spoils everything."

"I like it when she spoils everything. I like it when Miss Pimm gets mad at her and yells."

"Yeah, me too," and Rose Beth did her imitation of Miss Pimm. *"Look where you are going!"* she cried, making her eyes wide and pressing her front teeth tight together.

"And I like it when she stands there looking dumb."

"When who stands there looking dumb?" Daisy asked, coming up.

"Who do you think?"

"Goose?"

CHAPTER SIX

The Masked Ball

And now Mumma and Dada were invited to a ball, just like the one that the Pendletons attended, but this one was to be masked, and of course Mumma had no brocade dress to wear or a paisley shawl either. Certainly no tiara.

"There's going to be a masked ball?" Emmett asked. "Is that what you said?" and Lucie knew he was going to say something stupid, which he did, but not right away, because just at that moment Olive had one of her spells.

Olive was always having spells. One moment she would be standing in the kitchen, and the next she would topple to the floor. Lucie sometimes found her there when she arrived after school. "It's just one of my spells," Olive would explain as Lucie helped her up. Spills, Dada called them. "I hear you had one of your spills today, Olive," he would say, but Olive wouldn't see the joke. "It's *spells*," she would answer, if she answered at all. Once she had a spell all over again, right then and there, as soon as he had said that, and that was her answer.

"Oh, Olive," Mumma cried, "don't have a spell now," but it was too late. Olive was already on the floor, and everybody bent over her to look. "Let her be for a while," Mumma said, moving aside, and Emmett asked, "Let her be what?"

Lucie ignored Emmett. "How will you be masked, Mumma?" she asked, while they all waited for Olive to revive.

"It isn't *Mumma* who's to be masked," Emmett replied, finally getting to say his stupid thing. "It's the *ball*. It's a masked ball, Mumma said, not a masked person, right, Mumma? What kind will it be—basket or foot?"

Mumma didn't answer him. "Her color is coming back," she said, still bending over Olive.

"Where did it go?" Emmett asked, but Mumma didn't answer that either. "He just asks silly things to get attention," she always explained, "not because he really wants to know. Emmett is not a stupid boy, are you, Emmett?" But Lucie said, well, if he wasn't stupid, then he was ignorant, which was just as bad. That's what Miss Pimm said about Lucie all the time. "Lucie is not stupid," she would remind the class, when Emily or Rose Beth or Charlotte called her that. "She is *ignorant*. She is ignorant because she refuses to learn, and she refuses to learn because she is an *obstinate* child. Who can

40

tell the class the meaning of *obstinate*?" and Rose Beth would ask, "Ugly?"

"Her color didn't go anywhere, Emmett," Lucie told her brother now, pretending, like Miss Pimm, to be patient. "And a masked ball is a dance where everyone dresses up in disguise. They put on masks so no one will know who they are. What will you wear, Mumma?"

"Why don't you go as Mr. and Mrs. Babbidge?" Emmett suggested. "And everyone will think it's somebody else, dressed up to look like you."

"I think Olive is coming out of her spell now," Mumma said, ignoring Emmett again. "Her eyes are open."

"They were open all the time," Emmett pointed out.

"Yes, but she seems to be seeing through them now." Mumma bent at the waist to speak to Olive. "Olive, is your spell over?"

"Yes, Mrs. Babbidge, it is, but I need help in getting up." It was Lucie who set her to rights, and it was Lucie, too, who found the proper clothes for Mumma and Dada, but that wasn't until a whole lot later. Until after the new baby, in fact.

CHAPTER SEVEN

Vines

It was not in the blink of an eye, but a good seven days, before the miracle of the beans began to take place—the first miracle, that is. By next Tuesday morning, a stiff rubbery sprout of pale yellow-green had uncoiled in the center of every cup.

Every cup but Lucie's.

The soil in hers lay smooth and flat, like a tiny desert.

"Hey, Goosey-Loosey, what happened to your bean?"

"I bet she planted it upside down."

"Hey, yeah. Goose's bean is going to grow down instead of up."

"It's going to sprout in China."

"No, it's not. It's probably all shriveled up and dead."

"Yeah. Goose's bean is a corpse."

"Like *her*."

And two weeks after that, the vines were such a tangle that the cups could not be parted, one from the other, and the window shades could not be moved at all, up or down.

Lucie's soil was still bare, although she had sprinkled it each day when the pitcher came around.

"Not every bean contains the miracle of life," Miss Pimm finally told the class. "Lucie's bean was barren. Who can tell us the meaning of the word *barren*?"

Charlotte could. "It means your bean can't have babies."

"Lucie's bean did not germinate. It was infertile." Miss Pimm emptied Lucie's cup into her hand. "We will learn a lesson from it all the same. All experiments are useful, even those that fail. We will examine Lucie's infertile bean and try to discover why it did not develop. We will begin by exploring its interior structure." She flattened the hill of dirt and spread it around with the edge of her hand. "We will see what it has to tell us." But then, *"Lucie!"* she exclaimed. "Your bean is not here!" and indeed it was not.

"She ate it," Daisy whispered. "She swallowed it whole."

"It'll grow into a tree."

"It's growing already," and Anna lifted one of Lucie's thin braids. "It's all the way up to her ears! I can see the leaves!"

"It's going to grow clear out of her head!"

"It'll grow all the way up to the ceiling!"

"And a giant will live up there."

"Hey, Goose is going to have a giant living on top of her head!"

"I'm going to chop him down."

"I'm going to chop *her* down. Hey, Goosey-Loosey, look out! Here I come!"

CHAPTER EIGHT

Delia's Letter

Dear Lucie, (Strangely, miraculously, an answer had come from Delia Hornsby. Miss Pimm had held up the envelope that morning so everyone could inspect the foreign stamp with its dark-green queen.)

Your letter was a great surprise to me, Lucie read, smoothing the leaf-thin paper in her lap. *It was the first I'd ever had from America. I've never even been for a visit, so I couldn't think how my name got on your house. But then my father said it was my great-great-grandmother who must have put it there. She was the first Delia Hornsby. I'm the fourth, except I have a different last name, because of people getting married. Actually, I'm the fifth, if you count my great-aunt Bernadette who changed her name when she was seventeen because she thought it was too plain.*

My father says the first Delia Hornsby visited America when she was little. That's how we got the flag that's in our hall. She brought it back with her and it's been here ever since. The stripes have all gone grey, and the material is in shreds, but we keep it all the same. My father says you're not allowed to throw away a flag, even if it's American.

When I read your letter I went outside to see if the first Delia Hornsby had written her name on this house too, because she lived here a long time, but the only writing I could find was where Philip had put a vile word on the door. He's my brother and he's six. I'm twelve, and I'm not an interior designer. I go to school.

My house is not nearly as grand as yours, but it's nice all the same. Much nicer, anyway, than when we first moved in. You should have seen it then. Nobody had been living here since the first Delia died, and everything lay about in heaps. The chairs were upside down, and the piano keys wouldn't come back up when you hit them. And the carpets! Black from edge to edge, but then we beat out all the dust and there were flowers underneath. Roses mostly.

It took us months to put everything right, even after Francy came. She's our maid. Also, we have a lodger, Mr. Huggins. He lives in the attic, and he works in a hat shop all day, but he has his meals with us and we see him at the weekend.

Philip and I make fun of him behind his back. We tell what he looks like in his bath (Philip saw him once), and we make up dreadful stories about his past. My mother says we're nasty, and she's right. Do you do nasty things? Tell me what they are.

Yours faithfully,
Delia Hornsby Booth

CHAPTER NINE

Nasty Things

What nasty things had Lucie done? Not very many, come to think of it. Once, she and Emmett had removed Mr. Broome's hat from its peg and placed it, filled with apples, in the center of the tea table. That was probably nasty. "My hat has vanished from its peg!" Mr. Broome had cried at the time. *Vaneeshed*, is what he'd actually said, because Mr. Broome came from someplace far away; he never said where.

Lucie could write to Delia about that, and she could write, too, about the time she told Emmett that his head was going to fall off. "It will, Emmett," she had told him. "You must walk very straight and not look from right to left." Delia would think that was nasty too, although Lucie hadn't meant it to be nasty at all. She was simply being helpful. *Instructive*, Miss Pimm would call it. "I am not trying to insult, Lucie," Miss Pimm always said. "I am merely being *instructive* when I tell you that your face is never clean."

Mostly, though, they were nice to one another—

Emmett and Lucie, Mumma and Dada, and Olive—as nice as the Pendletons were, in fact. True, Lucie told Emmett all the time that he said stupid things, but she was being instructive then, too, and Olive said cruel things about the icebox, but that didn't count, because iceboxes have no feelings. Maybe if they had a lodger, she and Emmett could be nasty about him. Who could their lodger be?

Mr. Broome. Mr. Broome could be the lodger *and* the piano teacher. "That way," she would explain to Mumma, trying to persuade, "he could already *be* here on piano lesson day, and we wouldn't have to worry about letting him in." The last time he let himself in, he tripped on the rug and fell on Dada's umbrella. That's how it got broken and thrown in the churn. "Can we, Mumma? He could have the little room beneath the staircase." Not that that was a room, really; it was no more than a wedge of space behind a door, but Mumma would say yes just the same. Mumma said yes to nearly everything, just like Mrs. Pendleton. That was what was so wonderful about Mumma. And Dada would say yes, too. He would call the little room the Broome closet, and want a lodger there for that reason alone. "Mr. Broome is in his closet," he would say to Lucie. Dada made up things like that all the time, and that was what was so wonderful about *him*.

Maybe Emmett would get to see Mr. Broome in his bath.

Lucie could write all of that to Delia, if she wrote at all, which of course she wouldn't do.

CHAPTER TEN

Missing

Already there were seven letters from personages on the bulletin board: three from authors, one from an inventor, one from a mayor, one from a scientist, and one from Anna's uncle, who was the principal of a school. Also, one of the movie stars had replied, but not with a letter. He had sent Rose Beth a picture of himself with his signature across the lower right-hand corner. It didn't even say "Best wishes," but Rose Beth had tacked it on the bulletin board anyway, next to the letter from the inventor.

"And now we have a letter from Lucie's personage," Miss Pimm announced. "Share it with us, Lucie."

"I can't find it, Miss Pimm," Lucie said, slipping Delia's envelope with its strange green stamp beneath the notebook in her desk. Anyway, it was a sin to read other people's mail. Letters were inviolate.

"Lucie, I handed it to you only this morning."

"Yes, Miss Pimm," Lucie answered, her head inside her desk. "It's in here someplace."

"People who lose things," Miss Pimm told her, told

the class, too, "don't deserve to own them in the first place."

"Remember when she lost her shoes?" Daisy whispered.

"And she had to go to assembly in her boots?" Charlotte whispered back. "And one fell off during the salute?"

"Except she didn't call them boots; she called them something else."

"Galoshes."

"Galoshes! That's the most disgusting word I ever heard. It sounds like something animals eat."

"Like something swine eat," Claire put in.

"Like something *she* eats."

"Hey, yeah. Guess what Goose eats for breakfast every day. Galoshes."

"*Cream* of galoshes, with mushed-up bananas on top, and turnips."

"No, kale."

"Lucie," Miss Pimm said, "suppose there had been a sum of money in that envelope. Think what misery your carelessness would have caused."

"Yes, Miss Pimm. I'll find it in just a moment."

Later, as she crouched on the storeroom floor, the words of her classmates came from farther away, but they reached her all the same, floating down like snowflakes and settling on her shoulders and the rims of her ears.

"She's disappeared."

"Who?"

"Goose."

"Again?"

"Yeah, but this time it's during *school*."

"Does Miss Pimm know?"

"Not yet. She thinks she's in the library."

"Is she?"

"She was, but now she's gone. She's not in the bathroom, either."

"Let's tell."

"No, let's find her ourselves."

"Let's tie her up when we do."

"Oh, hey, yeah. Let's make her our prisoner. We'll tie her hands behind her back and put tape over her eyes. Then we'll lead her to Miss Pimm and ask for money. People do that. I saw it in a book once."

"Who would pay money for her?"

"Let's keep her for ourselves, then. She can be our slave."

"Oh, hey, a slave. I can make her bring me things on a tray."

"But where did she go?"

"The cellar, do you think?"

"No. Too scary."

"Where, then?"

The voices overhead died away and Lucie continued with her writing in the storeroom. "I have been in the interior design business for many years," she put down, making her writing look like someone else's. Like the huddled *b*'s and *k*'s of Delia's real letter, the one that lay in the bottom of Lucie's desk. "I design rooms in houses," she added. "I also make things to go into those rooms."

"Where have you been, Lucie?"

"In the bathroom, Miss Pimm."

"No, she wasn't, Miss Pimm. We looked. And she wasn't in the library either or the dining room."

"You were gone for over an hour, Lucie."

Over an hour? That's how long it had taken her to write that letter?

"What were you doing all that time, when you were supposed to be here in class?"

The bean vines at the window were a screen of grass-green tangles now: The jungle that Miss Pimm had promised had arrived, and the plants had been trans-ferred into long wooden troughs. Way, way over at the farthest edge, something stirred: something small and of the palest gray. A spider it was, so slender, so flossy, it might have been spun from its own sac of silk. It clung to a little green hook on a vine, and if

Lucie touched it with her finger, it would melt against her skin.

"Look at me, Lucie, when I speak to you. I am standing at my desk, not out the window."

"Yes, Miss Pimm."

"Where were you for over an hour when you should have been in class?"

"I was looking for my letter, Miss Pimm. The one from my personage, and here it is."

Of all the letters on the bulletin board, Lucie's was the only one written by hand and on loose-leaf paper. The others were all typed, on stationery that had a name and an address already printed across the top.

Dear Miss Babbidge, hers began, in the strange, cramped writing she'd made up.

Thank you for your letter of inquiry.

I will now answer your questions about my career.

I have been in the interior design business for many years. I design rooms in houses. I also make things to go into these rooms. The first interior I designed was for my very own house. It had a drawing room and dining room and kitchen downstairs. Upstairs, there were three bedrooms and a sewing room. There was also an attic. I made a lot of things for my house. I made the curtains and the rugs and the tablecloths. Also the pillows for the couch and the blue scarf that goes on the piano.

There's this very nice family living in that house now, and they still use the things that I made.

I very much hope that I have adequately answered your questions about my career, and I wish you every success in whatever career you choose for yourself.

Yours faithfully,
Delia Hornsby

"Goose's personage wrote the same exact words at the end of her letter that my personage wrote in his," Enid observed.

"Except for the *Yours faithfully* part," Daisy said.

CHAPTER ELEVEN

Quoits

"When is Mumma coming home?" Lucie asked, following Olive into the kitchen.

Olive turned to the clock. "At half past," she answered. "Half past on the dot is what your mother said."

"It's half past on the dot now," Lucie pointed out, "and she isn't home yet."

"No, she's not," Olive agreed. "But it will be half past on the dot when she comes through that door, just you wait and see."

Olive and Lucie said this to each other every time Mumma was out, and Olive was always right. But so was Lucie, because in fact the hands on the clock never moved; it was that kind of clock. And "half past on the dot" is what Mumma said when she came back home, a paper shopping bag hanging from her wrist.

"What did you bring us, Mumma?" Emmett asked, suddenly appearing at the top of the stairs.

"Something very nice." Mumma led the way into the drawing room. "It's a game, but first let me show you what I bought for myself." She let the shopping bag slip onto the floor, and she leaned over its open end. "Look!" and she held up a length of brown cloth.

"What is it," Emmett asked, "a flag?"

"No, Emmett," Lucie said. "It's a shawl, can't you tell? I think it's very pretty, Mumma, and it will keep your neck all warm."

"I don't think it's pretty at all," Emmett said. "Look, it has chalk stains on one side and there's a hole."

"Never mind," Mumma said. "It's only meant to be worn around the house."

"Around the house!" Emmett cried. "I thought it was to be worn around your *neck!*"

"Emmett, stop being silly," Lucie said. "Look, Mumma, it has all these pretty designs on it. I'm sure it's paisley. Maybe you could wear it to the masked ball."

"Maybe it could be the mask," Emmett suggested. "And you could look through the holes. What is the game you brought for us, Mumma? Is it something we can cheat at?"

"No, Emmett, it is not. And anyway, cheating isn't fair."

"Yes it is, if we all cheat at the same time. What game is it, Mumma?"

"It's called quoits," Mumma said. "It's a brand-new game."

"Quoits?" Emmett repeated. "What are they?" Lucie, of course, already knew, but she didn't say how. "It's ringtoss, Emmett."

Mumma reached into the bag and removed the spike on its disk and the five white rings to aim at it. "See? You play like this." She sailed a ring toward the spike across the floor, but it landed on the keyboard of the piano instead.

"Let me try," Emmett said. He stood a bit closer to the spike, but his ring floated to the piano, too.

"Take them back, Mumma. They're no good," he complained.

"What's no good?" Dada was suddenly at the door, although no one had heard his steps outside the house.

"Mumma bought us quoits, Dada. They're ringtoss, but there's something wrong with them. They're supposed to go on the spike, but they go on the piano instead."

"Well, then," Dada said. "We will have to change the rules. The rules are that you have to hit the piano."

"But then what is the spike for?" Mumma asked.

"For aiming at. You aim at the spike and the ring goes to the piano." And that is how they played. First Dada, and then Mumma, Emmett, and Olive all sailed their rings in the air and watched them land on the piano, or at least nearby.

Lucie's ring, though, flew across the room and settled magically on the slender silver prong.

Everyone was silent for a long while.

"Oh, Lucie," Mumma cried. "How did you do that?"

"I don't know, Mumma."

"Lucie always wins at games," Dada said. "It's her way."

"But Dada," Emmett pointed out, "she didn't win. She *lost*. You have to hit the *piano*. That's what you said. Those are the rules."

CHAPTER TWELVE

The Poem

Recitation was the last class of the day and it came every Tuesday, right after arithmetic. Sometimes Miss Pimm called it Poetic Discourse.

"Who has Stanza One?" Miss Pimm asked today.

Lucie had Stanza One, but she waited for someone else to point that out to Miss Pimm. It was Rose Beth who finally did. "Lucie does, Miss Pimm."

Everyone, of course, already knew that. The first stanza was the one that nobody wanted. It was the only stanza in the whole poem that was not about love. "Love!" Daisy had cried out in surprise the week before when the poetry books had been handed out. "This poem's all about *love!* Listen to *this*:

> "For a breeze of morning moves,
>   And the planet of Love is on high,"

and she laughed the way she and all the rest laughed when they discovered bad words on the playground fence. "This whole poem is about *love!*"

But they were not to take notice of that. "We are to

60

concern ourselves with the music of the verses," Miss Pimm told them, "not with their meaning. Listen, class," and she began to recite: "*Come into the garden, Maud, For the black bat, night, has flown.* I will say that line again," and she did, emphasizing the beat with a piece of chalk against her desk. "*For the black bat, night, has flown.* What do you hear, class, when I speak those words?"

"The chalk?" Emily asked.

"The black bat?" Daisy tried, but no; they heard the plucking of the strings of a violin: pluck, pluck, pluck. "Recite it with me, class. Deep breath, first. How do we breathe when we recite poetry? Rose Beth?"

"From the stomach, Miss Pimm."

"From the abdomen. Now, then. Sharpen your tongues and stiffen your lips and listen to the click of the consonants. *Begin!*"

To the tap of Miss Pimm's chalk, everyone recited with a nice sharp tongue and stiff lips, so that the words became the plucking of a violin string. Everybody except Lucie, whose lips remained thin and still and whose tongue had just discovered a bump on her palate that hurt deliciously when it was pressed.

"I can't hear you, Lucie," Miss Pimm said, stopping the class.

"That's because she isn't reciting, Miss Pimm," Claire explained.

"Recite the lines alone, Lucie," Miss Pimm ordered.

"I can't find them in my book, Miss Pimm."

"I know where they are, Miss Pimm," Emily said. "Should I recite them for her?"

At the end of the lesson, everybody had picked a stanza to memorize for today. Rose Beth had picked the part about the young lord-lover, and three girls had picked the part that went,

> My dust would hear her and beat,
> Had I lain for a century dead;
> Would start and tremble under her feet,
> And blossom in purple and red.

"He lets her walk on top of him; that's how much he loves her," Daisy had said.

"Also, she puts flowers all over him," Charlotte had added. Miss Pimm had assigned Lucie Stanza One, the one about Maud and the black bat, night, because no one else wanted it. Claire had picked the part about the passion-flower.

"Lucie?" Miss Pimm called now. "We will begin with you. Come to the front of the room."

"Yes, Miss Pimm." Lucie rose from her seat and walked down the aisle until she came to the blackboard, and then she turned to face the room.

In a moment, less than a moment, a tiny sting, sharp

as a pin, would strike her throat and make her cough. It struck, no matter what, each time she was called before the class. The cough, coming faster and faster, would grow loud, soft, loud again, and do nothing to drive away the sting that nipped at her throat like a bug.

Her mother, that long-ago day on the beach, had taken her by the hand and led her, carefully, backward into the sea. "Keep your back to the waves," her mother had cautioned, and Lucie had done that, letting the water slam against her head, liking the way that felt, liking the way it almost hurt but didn't. Liking, too, the patches of foam that froze to her shoulders, to her wrists, and in an eye-blink died away. And then, without warning, there came a wave that threw her down, threw her mother down, too, and when she opened her eyes she saw her own arms and legs, and her mother's as well, tangled up and swirling like a knot of rope that wouldn't come undone.

When finally she rose, it was to a beachful of faces, grinning, very likely, but maybe not; it was hard to tell, blurred as her eyes were with prickling mist. It was hard to yell, too, what with all that ocean in her throat and up her nose. All she could do was cough.

Now, each time she stood before the class, with the blackboard rising like a wave behind her, something sharp caught in the lining of her throat and she began to cough, to choke really: She couldn't draw a breath and water flooded her eyes so that she couldn't see the faces that grinned from all the desks.

"You are not breathing through your abdomen, Lucie."

She wasn't breathing at all. Something—a mosquito, it felt like, or a gnat—was biting at the corner of her throat, and if she swallowed hard it might wash away, but there was nothing to swallow, not even the cold juice that she could sometimes suck from inside her cheek.

"Look what she's doing. She looks like a fish."

"Lucie, stop feigning illness. Did you memorize your stanza?"

No, Miss Pimm, she tried to say.

"She never memorizes her lines, Miss Pimm," Rose Beth said. "When all the rest of us are rehearsing, she just looks out the window. She doesn't even take her book with her after class. It just lays in her desk."

"*Lies,* Rose Beth."

"No, it's *true,* Miss Pimm. I've seen it. She *hates* poetry. She thinks it's stupid. She said so once. I heard her." Rose Beth turned to Claire. "She thinks everything is stupid."

"She's stupid herself," Claire whispered back.

"Think of the name of the poem, Lucie," Miss Pimm

said. "The name of the poem is the first line of your stanza." When Miss Pimm spoke to Lucie, lots of times she sounded like the phrases in a workbook: "When you see the term 'percent,' think 'per hundred.' Twenty percent of a class means twenty students *per hundred* students."

"Surely you can remember the name of the poem, Lucie?"

The liquid in her eyes, stinging now like sea water, began to creep along the edges of her face.

"She's crying," Enid whispered.

"It's 'Come into the Garden, Maud,' " Claire said aloud, raising her hand, but not waiting to be called on.

"Repeat that, Lucie," Miss Pimm said.

Lucie's voice squeezed itself out between two coughs. "It's come into the garden, Maud," she croaked.

"Lucie, you are being deliberately impertinent." Miss Pimm bent over her roll book and entered into it a mark of some kind in red ink. "Return to your desk."

"Yes, Miss Pimm." Words came out at last.

"And you will see me after school."

Lucie stopped halfway down the aisle of desks. After school? *Today?*

CHAPTER THIRTEEN

Piano Day

But today was Tuesday—piano day—the best day of the week, when Mr. Broome came to give his lessons, and Lucie and Emmett got to wear their best clothes.

It wasn't really *lessons* that Mr. Broome gave, because he didn't exactly teach, but he called himself their teacher, and they called him that, too. Instead he gave *recitals*, and it wasn't he who gave them; it was Lucie and Emmett.

That was what was so wonderful about that day. Every Tuesday afternoon, first Lucie and then Emmett, dressed in their very special clothes, would enter the drawing room, march across the rug, and with one hand resting on the piano, announce in a good strong voice the name of the piece they had prepared all week.

"Chaconne by Bach," Lucie would recite, and then she would settle herself on the little piano bench and run her fingers back and forth across the keys.

Mr. Broome would simply rest his head against the wall and, with his lips turned up and his eyes half closed, stand very still and listen. Or *seem* to listen; no one could tell. Emmett said he was probably asleep.

Emmett never had his recital suit on when Mr. Broome arrived. "Emmett," Mr. Broome always had to remind him, "when you give a recital, you must honor your music and your listeners by wearing proper attire."

"Wearing a proper tire?" Emmett always answered, although he knew very well what Mr. Broome had said and, in fact, would already be hopping up the stairs, both feet together on each step, to get his clothes. In another minute he'd be shouting, "Lucie, help me with my buttons!"

Lucie's recital clothes were always lying across her bed, waiting for her when she came home from school, and she put them on right away. The petticoat was difficult, with its tiny hook and eye, but the dress slipped on quite smoothly—arms first, head next, chest, waist, and knees. The bow in the back was simple, too, as it was already stitched into place.

"Lovely!" Mr. Broome always exclaimed, as she entered the drawing room at last. "Lovely," but Lucie pretended not to notice. A performer never acknowledges remarks from the audience. That was one of Mr. Broome's rules, and so she'd simply bow and, in a voice never interrupted by coughs, announce, "Chaconne by Bach," as though hundreds of listeners were in the room. Mumma would straighten up on the sofa, Olive would lower her arms, and Mr. Broome, with his eyes half shut across his cheeks, would rest his head against the wall and listen, maybe.

CHAPTER FOURTEEN

After School with Miss Pimm

"You distress me, Lucie."

"Yes, Miss Pimm." Miss Pimm was going to be helpful today. Her eyes would not show white around the top when she said "I *never*," and her teeth would not catch on her lip. She wouldn't even say "I never." She rarely did when she spoke to Lucie alone. She would say, "I am trying to be helpful," instead. She would offer Lucie advice that would serve her in later life.

"When I assign an exercise, Lucie, it is not merely to fill your idle hours. Pick your head up when I speak to you. My exercises, Lucie, if properly executed, have an effect that will last throughout your lifetime. Keep your hands in your lap. You may not see the value of memorizing and reciting poetry now, but there will come a time in later years when you will be grateful for your training here at Norwood Hall and you will remember me for it. I am telling you this, Lucie, to be helpful."

"Yes, Miss Pimm."

The Adventures of the Pendletons lay on the desk, face-

up, and there on the cover were the Pendletons themselves, all of them: Mother and Father side by side on
a garden bench; Frank and Josie at their feet. Frank
held a little boat, Josie a doll. Lucie remembered the
episode in the book: They had just finished a picnic
beneath a yellow weeping willow—there on the grass
was their blanket, and there were the lemon biscuits
and chilled lemonade—and now they were resting and
digesting their food. The artist had caught them just
in time; moments later a thunderstorm came up, and
nothing remained of the little family scene but the doll
Josie dropped in her flight across the lawn and the
distant picnic blanket near the tree.

"Look at me, Lucie. Many girls return years later to
thank me for their schooling at Norwood Hall. Some
of those girls were gifted, Lucie. Some were not. What
they all thank me for most, though, is the poetry they
were obliged to learn. Memorization strengthens the
brain, Lucie. Without proper exercise, the brain ceases
to function. It becomes dry and useless, like a fig. What
did I just say, Lucie?"

"Dry and useless like a fig, Miss Pimm." Was a fig
useless? Was it useless because it was dry? Did a brain
dry up to the size of a fig? Could you feel it roll around
inside your head?

"Memorization strengthens the mind, Lucie, and recitation strengthens the body. It toughens the vocal

cords and builds up the abdominal wall. Our country depends on men and women with strong voices and tough abdominal walls. And what does poetry itself strengthen?"

Not the mind or body. What else was there? "I don't know, Miss Pimm."

"Poetry strengthens the *soul*. Head up, Lucie. Poetry strengthens the soul. Always remember that. Why didn't you memorize your stanza?"

"I forgot, Miss Pimm."

"You failed to memorize it because you did not fully understand the value of memorization and recitation. Also, your mind is on other things. Look at me. What is your mind on, Lucie?"

"Other things, Miss Pimm."

"*What* other things?"

"I don't know, Miss Pimm. Nothing." Mumma and Olive would be in the drawing room by now, waiting, and Emmett would be standing in the hall. Mr. Broome would be at the front door, his hat still on his head, looking out. They would all be wondering where she was.

"You are not a gifted girl, Lucie, and your looks are plain. It does not profit such a person to disdain poetry. A person of few gifts and plain looks disdains poetry at her peril. Remember that always. What must you not disdain, Lucie?"

"Plain looks, Miss Pimm."

"*Poetry*. Fill your soul with poetry, Lucie, and you will be forgiven your looks. You may go now."

"Yes, Miss Pimm."

CHAPTER FIFTEEN

Delia's Second Letter

Dear Lucie, Delia wrote, although her first letter had brought no reply.

I forgot to tell you that I have a pet, too. It's a cat, not a bird, and its name is Mutt, which is short for muttonchops, because that's what he likes to eat. Francy trips over him all the time. She trips over him even when he isn't there. She just falls down for no reason at all and says it's because of the cat. My father thinks it's very funny when she falls. "Just come back from a trip?" he asks her, while she's getting up, but she doesn't see the joke. "It's the cat got in my way," she tells him.

Mr. Huggins falls sometimes, too, but not the way Francy does. Once he fell coming in the front door, and he had to wear a plaster on his head for a week. Philip said he looked like a balloon with a patch.

Let's tell each other things that we hate. Here's mine: I hate it when hair grows in people's ears. Also, I hate it that you can't be however old you want. I'd pick thirty if I could. Here's what else: I hate it that someday today is going to be olden days. Do you hate that, too? Do you hate it that a long time from now people are going to laugh at everything we do today? They're all going to look at our toothbrushes and everything in a museum somewhere and say, "Ooh, look what they used to brush their teeth with!" I hate that, so here's what I do: I put notes all around the house that say, "I think this is all very stupid." Then all those people will laugh at everybody else but not at me. What do you think they'll laugh at most? I think roller skates.

Also, guess what. My mother is going to have a baby.

Please write back.

Let's be friends forever.

Yours faithfully,
Delia

CHAPTER SIXTEEN

The New Baby

"They're not home yet," Emmett called down from the upstairs hall, as Lucie came through the front door.

"Of course they're not," Olive answered from the kitchen. "Your father said after teatime, which can't be for a while, as it hasn't yet begun," and she moved around the table in those long, slow hops of hers. "Come into the kitchen, both of you. That's where tea is being served."

"In the kitchen!" Emmett exclaimed. "Why not in the drawing room?"

"Because your mother will be coming home very soon with her baby."

"*Her* baby!" Emmett turned to face Olive. "I thought it was to be all of ours."

"It's hers to begin with," Olive explained. "After that it will be everybody's, and then after *that*, it will be its own."

"That means never," Emmett said. "It will always be the baby, because that's what it is. Why must we have tea in the kitchen?"

"It's because of the crumbs. We can't have crumbs on the drawing room floor. Everything must be clean for the baby."

"I see," which is what Emmett often said when he was about to say something stupid. "Even the crumbs?"

"Emmett," and now Olive's voice was beginning to rise just a little, "if you are not quiet, I shall have one of my spells."

"Behave yourself, Emmett," Lucie scolded now. "We can't let Olive have one of her spells today."

"Well, then she can have one of mine," and he liked what he said so much that he fell off his chair.

Olive said later that if Emmett hadn't been making so much noise in the kitchen, they would have heard Mumma and the new baby coming home, but Emmett didn't believe that. "They were probably home all along," he said. "They had probably sneaked upstairs long before, to surprise us." Anyway, when Dada called out, "We're here!" it was from the upstairs hall, not the front door, and Mumma was . . ."Where?" Lucie and Emmett cried out, as they flew up the stairs.

"In here." Mumma's voice was faint behind her door. "Come and see," Dada said, and he led the way in. Lucie followed, and then came Emmett, with Olive last of all.

Mumma was wrapped from neck to ankle in her new

brown shawl, "Looking like a cigar," Emmett said later. Right now, though, he didn't say a word. No one did. They all held very, very still.

"Is it a boy or a girl?" Emmett finally asked.

"It's a girl," Mumma answered.

"Will it speak English?"

"Yes, Emmett, of course. When it learns to speak."

"Then it is lucky it was born here," he answered, "and not in France, where no one would understand a word it said."

"Emmett, don't be silly," Olive scolded, and then they all began to move, one behind the other, to the sewing room where the cradle had already been set up.

"What's its name?" Emmett asked along the way.

Lucie, of course, already knew: It was the most wonderful, the most beautiful name she had ever heard in all her life—the most beautiful name, in fact, in the world.

She slipped her hand into her pocket then and, reaching through the open wall of the house, very carefully dropped the new family member into its tiny, tiny bed. "There she is," Mumma said, and they all bent over to gaze at the ivory-white head with its tiny red face: an eye, an eye, a mouth—dot, dot, circle.

"And its name is Maud." But it wasn't Mumma who spoke those words, it was Lucie.

PART TWO

PART TWO

CHAPTER SEVENTEEN

The Dollhouse

The real Lucie, that is, not the four-inch one with the white china face and the little wire loops at the elbows and the knees.

The *real* one: Goosey-Loosey, with the thin brown braids and the dull plain looks, who lived at Norwood Hall with fifty other girls and who got everything wrong and whose face was never clean and who lost everything, even her shoes once, and who never memorized her lines and who hated poetry and who disappeared each day, nobody knew where.

The *real* Lucie who, every afternoon, when the clock said three and classes were done, took a sudden quick turn down a dark hidden stair and locked herself inside a room where no one went. A storeroom must have been what it was called, but that, of course, could not be right. There was nothing stored inside it but the dollhouse. And even that was not quite *stored*, since no one even knew that it was there.

No one but Lucie: She'd discovered it one morning two years before while hiding in the cellar from her teacher. The door was unmarked and the room behind it dark, and she'd banged her knees on something like a milk crate.

She had hidden there all day, while voices called her name from above, but it wasn't until late afternoon, when the light spilled through the window and trickled on the floor, that she got to see the crate for what it was: a full-size dollhouse, three stories high, with tiny-patterned walls and wood-plank floors and a stairway with a rail smooth as steel.

Its furnishings lay in heaps in every room. Sticks and bits of rag were all they seemed to be at first, but Lucie smoothed them out and stood them right side up, and there all at once was a piano; there on the floor was a rug.

"It's like real," she had said, half aloud, half not. And it was, in a way: The knocker on the door made a tiny, quick rap when she let it fall against the wood, and the bricks on the chimney were rough against her thumb. "It's even got a toilet," she had said, to herself this time, "with a flush thing on top."

But no real house is missing its entire back wall, and no real people living in it have arms and legs of china and heads whose hair and faces are painted on. "This one will be the mother," Lucie had said when she found

the four small figures lying facedown in the space beneath the stairs. "And this will be the father, and these
will be their little boy and girl."

She named the mother Mumma and the father Dada,
which is what some children called their parents in a
book she knew. Emmett's name came from a song—a
lullaby she'd learned in music class. The girl doll's name
would have to wait: Lucie could think of nothing that
was right.

She hopped the mother doll up and down and spoke
for it deep inside her own head. "I'm Mumma," she
made it say. "My clothes are all mussed up, but that's
because I've been sleeping in them all this time, so you
must pay them no mind." ("Pay them no mind" was
what people said in that same book, and that was how
the dolls all talked in the beginning. Now, of course,
they all spoke like the Pendletons—except for Olive,
who usually spoke like Miss Pimm—and had the same
adventures, too, some of the time.)

Mumma's clothes *were* mussed up, and one of her
arms was hanging loose, but her china hair was smooth
and her clothes, though all in wrinkles, were very
lovely clothes all the same: a pink satin dress that came
down to her heels and a scarf sort of thing around her
neck; painted black shoes and, underneath the dress,
a frail white frill of brittle lace.

Lucie lifted off the scarf and held it to the window. It was pale—sky pale—and thin as the wing of a cicada; if she pressed it, it would turn to blue-gray powder on her thumb. "Give that back," she made the mother doll say. "This room is full of damp," and Lucie draped the scarf on her shoulders once again.

"And I am Dada." Lucie held the father doll by its waist as he introduced himself all around. Parents shouldn't have to explain who they are to their own families, Lucie knew, but she thought it best in this case, as they'd all been asleep beneath the stairs for so long. How long? she wondered. Years, maybe; dust lay on every surface, like snow. She blew across the roof and a tiny gray blizzard flew about.

"My clothes aren't quite as mussed as Mumma's," Dada went on, in his voice inside Lucie's head, "because they weren't quite so mussable to begin with," and that seemed true: He wore narrow black pants, a tight gray jacket, and a hat made of something very stiff. His umbrella was attached to his cuff.

"Come, children," he said to the boy doll, to the girl doll. "Let's get busy around here. Look what a mess we all are in."

Lucie lifted up the two small dolls and shook them out. "Stop that!" she made them cry, one after the other, as their heels clicked together and their wired arms swung. "I'm only getting you clean," she told them. "Just look at what you look like." Mrs. Henderson, the housemother at Norwood Hall, said that to Lucie all the time, and it seemed like a good thing to say to the dolls: "Just look at what you look like," and what they looked like was not particularly nice. The girl doll's dress had become thin as paper, and it cracked at every crease and at the hem. A wide yellow blot stained the boy doll's shirt, and the color of his pants, Lucie knew, was not what it had started out to be.

Also, both their faces were thick with sticky grime. Lucie licked her thumb and wiped them clean. "Don't do that!" she made them yell, as she scraped around their noses with her nail. "Be still," Lucie told them. "He that hath clean hands," she recited, although it wasn't their hands she was cleaning, "and a pure heart," she continued, although clearly they had no hearts at all, "shall ascend into the hill of the Lord." Mrs. Henderson said that, too, shouting it each morning into the lavatory as everyone was washing up for breakfast.

Lucie found what must have been a sofa, and she seated all the dolls upon it in a row. "We have to fix this place up," she told them, and the father doll agreed. "It's a mess," he said again. "Look at that table. It's upside down, and the piano has a leg that isn't there."

"And the birdcage!" The girl doll cried. "It's been knocked onto the floor, with the bird all dead."

"It isn't dead," Lucie told her, blowing dust from a wad of green fluff. "It is only asleep. Watch this. *Sing, bird*," and she sang for it with three high tweets. "See? It's perfectly alive."

"I want it for my room," the girl doll said, but the boy doll wanted it for his, and soon they were having a fight. "It's mine." "No, it's *mine*!" they shouted at each other inside Lucie's head. "It's hers," Lucie announced. "I'll find something nice for you in just a minute, Emmett," and she did. "Oh, look at *these*," she cried. "It's a bunch of teeny animals. It's a Noah's ark! Look, Emmett, they can go two by two. You can have them for your room. This can be your room, with the stripes on the walls. And"—she lifted the girl doll by its waist, —"this one with the flowers and the alcove is for you. I'll put the birdcage over here in the corner, and this can be your bed. I'll make a nice new spread for it, and a canopy, too, to attach to these posts. And I'll fix up these curtains so they look nice, and this can be your rug. Look, it has flowers on that you can see when you scratch this stuff all off."

It was then that Lucie thought of the name she'd give the doll. "This room will be for you, Lucie," she said, "because it's going to be so beautiful. Beautiful like you."

"We must have a party," the mother doll said from the sofa, "as soon as everything is all fixed up. And *I'll* be the one to make the canopy."

"But I have nothing to wear to a party," the girl doll—Lucie—said, "except this disgusting old dress."

"*Lucie!*"

"And I hate these pants," Lucie made the boy doll say. "They make my knees show. My knees are ugly."

"*Lucie!*"

Lucie stood up. The *real* Lucie. "I have to go," she said to the four china dolls on their couch.

"*Lucie!*"

"I'll be back another day," she told them. "You stay right here."

"*LUCIE!*" The voices from upstairs began to float through the walls.

"Where'd she go?"

"Who?"

"Goose. She's been gone all day."

"Goose is gone? Where'd she go?"

"No one knows. Mrs. Henderson says she wasn't here for lunch."

"Maybe she fell out a window."

"Maybe she's dead."

"No, she's not. There she is—over there."

"Hey, Goose, where were *you*?"

"Look at that dirt all over your face. Where'd you go?"

"Just look at what you look like, Lucie Babbidge. Where *were* you?"

"Visiting, Mrs. Henderson."

CHAPTER EIGHTEEN

In the Dormitory

"There's nothing here but this." Daisy lifted a comb from Lucie's nightstand drawer.

"Ooh, disgusting," Charlotte said. "Dizz *gusting*. It's got sticky stuff all over its teeth."

"So has Goose. She's got sticky stuff all over *her* teeth."

"Hey, I bet this *is* her teeth. I bet she takes them out at night and puts them in her drawer."

"And when she gets up in the morning, she combs her hair with them."

"Yeah, and after that, she puts them in her mouth."

"Swine," Claire said.

"What else is in there?"

"Crumbs only. From some old piece of bread, it looks like."

"Check her locker."

But Rose Beth's new handkerchief that her uncle had sent her for her birthday, the peach linen handkerchief that was embroidered all around with lace and that Rose Beth said she would never blow her nose in as long as she lived because it was so beautiful, was not in Lucie's locker either.

Nothing was in Lucie's locker, in fact, except two dark dresses and her sweater, the one with only three buttons left and the sleeves rubbed pale at the elbow. Also, on the floor, her galoshes.

All the other lockers were crammed with things, and the nightstands, too. Jane's nightstand was so crowded, she had to keep her tissue box under her bed. Lucie's tissue box stood alone on her nightstand, filled to the top, but with tissues that were used. And everything in her locker had come from the hand-me-down box in the closet where Mrs. Henderson kept the brooms and mops and the gallon cans of cleanser that gave Norwood Hall its smell.

The Pendletons called *their* outgrown clothes "reach-me-downs" and sent them along to their servant's little niece, who was never seen at all, but who wore all of Josie's old clothes—and some of Frank's besides: shirts that everyone called jerseys, and gloves and hats and stockings. Everyone wore stockings in that book, even Frank. "So you won't suffer from chilblains when the weather turns cold," their mamma always said.

Hand-me-down. Who was the *me* in that phrase? Lucie wondered. Who told somebody, *Hand me down?* The sweater itself? The dark-green sweater with the see-through elbows that Lucie wore each day and sometimes, too, at night, when her bed was icy cold? Did it say to some long-ago girl, *Hand me down? Hand me down to someone, please, so I won't have to spend the rest of my life on this closet floor with these cans of cleaning stuff? Hand me down,* maybe, *to Lucie Babbidge when she comes to Norwood Hall, since she's the only one who'll ever put me on?*

"Try her bed," Rose Beth said. "Look at all those lumps. I bet that's all the stuff she's been stealing. I bet my handkerchief's in there."

But the lumps were Lucie's socks, and her underclothes, too. She dressed and undressed beneath her blanket, not out in the aisles between the beds, like everybody else, and she kept all her things beneath the sheets.

"Let's hide all this stuff and put something else in here instead."

"Something repulsive," Anna suggested.

"What's more repulsive than what's already there?" Emily asked. "What's more repulsive than Goose's underwear?"

No one knew, but Claire squeezed a curlicue of toothpaste on the sheet just the same. "She'll think it's something dead and all squashed into goo when she sticks her feet down her bed."

"That's what she gets for stealing Rose Beth's hanky."

"Where did she put it, anyway?"

"Look under the mattress. I bet that's where it is."

"I don't see anything," Charlotte said after a while, and she let the mattress fall back crooked on the bed-spring. "I don't see a thing."

What she also didn't see was Lucie herself, who'd been watching all along from the unused locker in the corner, peering through the four narrow slots in its gray metal door.

CHAPTER NINETEEN

Lucie's Song

Lucie closed the storeroom door behind her and pulled on the string she'd discovered long ago, the one that made a ceiling light go on. Then she spread her sweater on the floor and knelt on it in front of the dollhouse. The little china doll was resting beside the doorframe, just where Lucie had left her the day before. With a poke from the doll's tiny finger, the door swung open, and Lucie moved the doll inside. "Olive!" she said for it in her head. "Olive, Olive, *Olive*! I'm home from school!"

And now Lucie moved around to the other side of the house, the side that had no wall, so she could reach in and move everything about. A clothespin with a pipe cleaner twisted just below its knob lay on the floor beside a toy wooden churn. "Oh, Olive," the girl doll said in Lucie's silent voice, "you've had another spell." Lucie took the doll's hands in her own fingers and lifted the clothespin with them. "There, now," she made the doll say, as together they leaned the clothespin against a small iron stove. "You're all recovered."

"That's *hot!*" Lucie made the clothespin cry.

"Oh, Olive, I forgot." Lucie changed to the girl doll's voice in her head and moved Olive over to a wall, just beneath the clock—the one whose single hand hung forever at half past. "And Olive, just look at what you look like," the doll continued. "Your hat got knocked off your head when you had your spell, and your dress got mussed." Lucie herself fastened the hat back on Olive's head, but she made the girl doll smooth Olive's black crepe-paper skirt.

"Where's Emmett?" the girl doll said. "It's piano lesson day."

"He's getting up from his nap," Olive told her.

Lucie now reached up to the second level of the house and removed from one of its rooms another little doll held together at its joints by wire pins.

"No, I'm not!" Lucie made him say, "I'm coming down from it," and she slid him down the narrow wooden stair.

"Don't say that all the time, Emmett," his china sister said to him. "It gets tiresome after a while."

"I'm not saying it," Lucie answered for him. "I'm just thinking it out loud."

"Lucie!" Mumma was calling from the drawing room. "Come and tell me what you did in school today," and Lucie hopped the girl doll into the big room next to the stairway.

The drawing room was crammed with things. Most of them had come with the dollhouse and were quite old: the rug, all edged in fringe; the piano with its painted row of keys; the straight-backed velvet sofa where Mumma liked to sit. Some things, though, were not old at all. Four recent portraits hung on the walls. Three were of Presidents and one was of a queen. They were no bigger than postage stamps. They *were* postage stamps. Lucie had pasted them there herself. The queen one was from Delia's second letter. The others had come from other people's personages. One leg of the piano was new; it was a piece of yellow pencil that Lucie had broken in two. The baby's cradle was new—a deep walnut shell, scraped clean and polished to a shine with crayon wax. And of course the quoits neatly stacked on the piano were new—five reinforcements and a sharp thin tack.

"School was lovely today, Mumma." Lucie bent the girl doll's legs and seated her beside her mother on the sofa. "My teacher invited me to tea after class so we could talk."

"Tell me about it," the mother doll said. Lucie lifted the mother doll's arm just enough so that it rested on the little girl's shoulder. Her other arm lay on her pink satin lap. With the toe of a glazed china shoe, she gave the walnut cradle a tiny tap, making it rock once, twice.

"She said I had the best speaking voice in the whole class, Mumma. She said I was gifted."

Olive appeared at the doorway just then. "Did you bring the ginger cookies, Olive?" Mumma asked.

"Oh, Madam, I clean forgot." Olive always said she clean forgot things. "She also forgot to clean," Dada sometimes said, bending over the grate where bits of dust still lay.

"And put the kettle on, too," Mumma reminded her.

"Oh, yes, Olive," Emmett said. "Do put the kettle on. It would make a lovely hat. Don't you think, Lucie?"

The china Lucie, he meant, not the real one kneeling on the storeroom floor. The dolls never spoke to the real Lucie, not ever at all, nor she to them. They addressed only each other, inside her head.

"That isn't the least bit funny," the china girl said.

"It wasn't meant to be," her brother told her back.

A little mewing cry sounded suddenly, and Mumma rocked the cradle once again with her toe.

"Oh, Mumma," the girl doll said. "May I hold her in my lap?"

"Yes, of course you may. She's been crying for you all day."

Lucie lifted the bean from its walnut shell and laid it on the girl doll's knee. "Don't cry, Maud," she made the girl doll say. "I'm here to hold you now and to make you feel all nice. Here, you can suck on my finger, if you like." Lucie touched the tip of the doll's china hand to the little painted circle on the bean. "And I'll sing you your own special song. Ready? Here it is: *Come into the garden, Maud, For the black bat, night, is flown, Come into the garden, Maud, I am here at the gate alone.*" Lucie made up a tune for the doll to sing, and she continued to sing until she had finished the poem, all eleven verses. "Do you like that, Maud? It's all about you," and the doll rocked the bean some more.

"Oh, Lucie!" Mumma cried. "That was the most beautiful song, and you sang it all by heart!"

"No, she didn't, Mumma," Emmett said. "She sang it by mouth. I could see."

CHAPTER TWENTY

In the Lunchroom

"What's *this*?"

"Mrs. Henderson says it's snow peas."

"Snopies? What's that?" Claire held a flat green pod up in the air.

"It's to eat," Enid said. "It's vegetables."

"But there's no peas inside. It's just pods."

"Yeah, well that's what you're supposed to eat. The pods. It has iron and stuff inside, Mrs. Henderson said."

"Eat the *pods*? But that's what you're supposed to throw *away*. That's what they give to pigs."

"To swine," Claire said. "They gave us swine food for lunch."

"Ooh, taste it. It's like wax paper. Hey, taste one, Daisy. It's green wax paper."

At the tip of each pod was a pale yellow tail. Lucie pinched one between her fingers and gave a tug. A long thin string uncoiled, clear as cellophane, and she held it with both hands to the lunchroom light. It stretched before her eyes like a stiff glass rod.

"Look what Goose is doing with *hers*. She's opening it up."

"Hey, look at *that*! It opens with a string you pull, like a Band-Aid. Hey, let's open it up and see what's inside."

"What *is*?"

"Dead pea stuff."

"Here comes Miss Pimm."

"Miss Pimm, Lucie's playing with her food again."

There were a dozen green strings in Lucie's hand by now, all slippery and smooth, and they hung like strands of grass from the sea. She wove them in and out among her fingers.

A man had been there, too, that long-ago day. Her father. "I'll make you a mermaid," he'd announced, and she'd stood there in the sun, waiting for him to fashion one from clay, from water, from whatever he could find—the warm thick air, it could be. But he'd meant what he had said: He would make *her* a mermaid, burying her legs in a tail of sculptured sand, molding scalloped scales with the arc of a shell, laying threads of seaweed in her hair.

"Wait, you'll need a mirror," he had added, "for gazing at your own deep-sea eyes," and he'd placed a polished clamshell in her hand. "And a comb, to straighten out the tangles on your blue-green head." A comb was hard to find. "You'll have to use your fingers," he finally had said, and she'd done just that, running her fingers through the long green shreds.

"And jewels, don't forget," he had gone on. He had hung a seaweed bracelet on each of her wrists and, around her neck, a stiff tangled plant of the sea: brown-black, rubbery, and filled with swollen beads. Lucie had tried to pop them with her nail, so they'd burst against her ear. But their skin was tough and slippery, and when at last she broke one with her teeth, it made no sound at all. Instead, an ooze of salty liquid stung her tongue, and she twisted to one side to spit it out.

She had stayed a mermaid in the sand all that afternoon, rippling the scales of her tail with her kneecaps, and squeezing the juice from the blue-green hair, watching it dry in the sun. The *sun!* That is what she remembered best of all. So flat it was, grinning like those happy yellow disks she always drew, with their wreaths of sharp-petaled hair. So far away. And yet, even then, as she wriggled in the sand, it had its eye on her and was reddening her shoulders, making plum skin of her back, with a fire she didn't know was there.

CHAPTER TWENTY-ONE

Snow

"CHARGE!" Emmett jumped into the drawing room with Dada's broken umbrella held like a sword between his hands. "Don't move or you'll be dead."

"Hush, Emmett," Mumma said. "You'll wake the baby." The bean baby still lay in the china Lucie's lap, fast asleep. "It's piano-recital day, and we'll want to get on with our tea. Put the umbrella down and help Olive set the table."

"Oh, yes, Mumma," he replied. "Where would you like me to set it? Over here on the rug or somewhere on my head?"

"Oh, Emmett, stop that," Mumma said, while Lucie herself—the real one—arranged the tea things on the table before the sofa: tiny flowered cups with saucers to match and spoons not much bigger than Mumma's fist.

All the tea things had been in the dollhouse from the start, but the food that went along with them was new each day. Lucie brought it in her pocket from her plate every lunch: crumbs, mostly, from pieces of bread, but other things too.

"All ready, Mrs. Babbidge." Olive stood at the doorway with a small kettle hanging from the loop of one pipe cleaner arm, and a flat oblong tray attached to the other. "Teatime," and she advanced smoothly across the room.

"It's a lovely tea, Olive," Mumma said, and Emmett bent at his hinged waist. "No, it's not," he said. "What's this green stuff on the tray?"

"It's snow peas," Olive answered.

"Snow peas! *Snow* peas? Oh, Olive, is that true? Is there really such a thing? Does it really snow peas sometimes? Does it? You get up one morning and you see it snowing *peas* outside? How very beautiful that must be. And does that mean it snows other things, too? Figs? Nice fat figs, going plop, plop, plop on the sill? Oh, Olive, if it did, I'd go outside with a shovel and make a figman."

"Don't be stupid, Emmett," his sister doll said.

"And an igloo," he went on.

"Emmett, I said stop."

"A figloo."

"Emmett!"

"And then I'd make a pigloo, if it started snowing pigs. Wouldn't that be nice, Lucie? I'm going to make up a poem about that," he went on. "Would you like to hear me say it? It goes *What would a pig—*"

"EMMETT!" The girl doll jumped up from the sofa so quickly that the bean fell from her lap and rolled across the rug, out of sight.

"Oh, Emmett, now look what you made me do. Mumma! The baby's *gone*! Where'd she *go*? Oh, *Mumma*!"

"I'll look," Olive offered, and she lay flat on the floor. "There she is," she called out at last. "Under the cabinet. We'll need a stick of some sort to bring her out."

"Dada's umbrella," Emmett cried, waving it. "Here, Olive."

"Emmett, it's all your fault," the girl doll said as Olive's pipe cleaner arm moved the umbrella back and forth under the cabinet. And then, when the bean finally rolled out onto the rug, she cried, "Oh, Mumma, look at her face! It's all spotted red. *Look* at her. She's got spots all *over*."

A little mewing sound came from the bean.

"Not *all* over," Emmett corrected, and he was right, but the baby was spotted all the same. The real Lucie's thumb had rubbed the bean when she'd helped to pick it up, and a pale red blur now smudged its cheek. "She's just red from crying so hard," and with that the mewing sound grew louder.

It stopped altogether, though, when the girl doll began to yell at her brother. "You *did* it, Emmett!" she cried. "Maud is spotted all over like a cow, and it's all your fault."

"No, it's not," he answered smoothly. "It's Olive's. She's the one who spotted her under the cabinet, isn't she, Mumma?"

But this time no one had a chance to tell Emmett to be quiet, because Olive had something to say. "Oh, come look, everybody," she called from the window. "Come *see*. It's *snowing!*"

CHAPTER TWENTY-TWO

The Surprise

And it was. Little white flakes were falling in a shower at the window, settling on the doorsill and the ledges and in Lucie's lap. The real Lucie's. She blew little puffs of air at the paper as it fell in shreds from her hands.

"Oh, look, everybody!" Emmett cried. "It's snowing! *Real* snow, too, not the pea kind or fig. Oh, Mumma, can we go out in it and play? Can we?"

"No, Emmett. You have no winter clothes," and that was true. Emmett had no outdoor clothes at all, but then he didn't need them, as he never left the house. "You'll get chilblains," she added, "if you go out now. See how fast the snow is falling." In fact, it was all coming down in a single clump.

"Well, then," Emmett said, "they should make snow out of something else. Something warm. They should make it out of wool."

"That's stupid, Emmett," the girl doll said, standing at the window beside her brother. "Look, Mumma, the snow is the kind that doesn't melt. It just stays where it has fallen, like drops of paint. See how beautiful it is."

Mumma held Maud up to the window so she, too, could see the scraps of snow that lay on the ground and didn't melt away. "It is beautiful," Mumma agreed. "Look, Maud. This is your first snow," but then she suddenly spun around. "Oh, dear!" she exclaimed. "What was *that?*"

Something had crashed in the front hall. Two things, as it turned out: a black plastic thimble and a clothespin. Not the clothespin that was Olive. The other one. This one's legs were painted black and so was the top of its knob. A face—two half-shut eyes like parentheses at rest and a small smile—had been drawn in marking pen above its neck.

"It's Mr. Broome!" the girl doll cried, spinning around from the window. She made it to the front hall in one long jump. "Oh, Mr. Broome, you've had another fall." She bent over and lifted the clothespin by its pipe cleaner arm. "And look what's become of your hat!" She fitted the thimble over the smooth round knob. "Poor Mr. Broome. Did you hurt yourself?"

Mr. Broome rested against the stair rail for a moment before answering. "Yes, I deed," he said. "I struck my head a blow. I struck eet a nasty blow." But before the girl doll could say anything else, he scolded, "You are not properly attired. Either of you," he added, as Emmett hopped in from the drawing room.

"We'll get dressed right away," the girl doll said, to keep Emmett from saying his dumb thing about a proper tire.

But there was Mumma, still holding Maud. "I forgot to tell you, Lucie," she said. "There's a surprise waiting for you in your room."

"Oh, Mumma, is there? A surprise in my room?"

"It can't be in your room," Emmett said. "The surprise will be in *you* when you see what it is."

The real Lucie hopped both dolls up the stairs without thinking up any reply for the girl doll to make, and she put Emmett into his room—the one with the striped paper on the walls—and then his sister into hers.

And there was the surprise. "Oh, Mumma!" the girl doll cried at the doorway. "Oh, Mumma, how *wonderful!*" There, stretched across the tall posts at each corner of her bed, was the canopy that Mumma had promised long ago to make, the most beautiful canopy the girl doll could imagine—woven of peach linen and hemmed in lace as fragile as ocean froth drying on the beach.

CHAPTER TWENTY-THREE

Delia's Third Letter

"You have another letter from your personage, Lucie. Would you like to read it to the class?" Miss Pimm held up another one of Delia's envelopes with the green queen staring out from the corner.

"It's not about her career anymore, Miss Pimm," Lucie said, taking the letter. "It's personal," and, wonderfully, Miss Pimm did not argue.

Dear Lucie,

It's odd, the things that happen in this house. Ever since we moved in, strange things have been going on. Good things, sometimes, and bad things, too. What's odd is that they happen by themselves. Does that ever happen in your house? The piano keys got clean one day, though my mother said she never touched them, nor Francy either. One day they were all smudged and sticky, and the next day they were shiny and smooth. "Smooth as satin," Francy said, but she was wrong. Satin makes dents when you touch it. These were smooth as teeth. They are teeth, Francy

*says. From an elephant. Did you know that? Elephants have this
row of black and white teeth. You could play tunes on them, if
you wanted, but then you'd have to put your hand inside the
elephant's mouth, and nobody wants to do that. That's why they
have pianos.*

*Our new baby came. Its name is Lizzie, and it was a surprise.
I knew it was supposed to come, but it was a surprise anyway.
I got home from school one day and there it was, all red and soft
and wrinkled up like a tomato that's been boiled.*

Let's like each other a lot.

When are you going to write back?

> *Your friend,*
> *Delia*

A snapshot was enclosed, of a family in front of a
house. They all stood in a straight row, their faces
made pale by too much light: a father, a mother, a
girl, and a boy. "This one's me," Delia had written in
ink against the sky, and an arrow, like a falling plane,
hung above the girl's head. None of their clothes fitted
right. You could see the boy's belly button below his
shirt. Navel, Mrs. Henderson called it. "I want to see
clean navels!" she shouted every Thursday night when
they all lined up for their showers. Miss Pimm told
them to say "umbilicus." "Call things by their proper
anatomical names," she told them, but no one ever did.
Mostly, they made up secret names that they whispered

to each other after dark and whose meaning Lucie only guessed at, when they reached her ears at all.

That would be Philip, the one with the belly button. Funny, that people who lived so far away—in a land not touching her own, or even touching another land that touched her own; a land a whole ocean away— should be formed just like people right here. With belly buttons. She brought the photograph up close to her eyes, so close that a second belly button sprang from the first and jumped to the edge of the scene.

The mother and father looked like mothers and fathers everywhere—tall, wide, and with faces you couldn't quite make out. As for Delia herself, she was not what Lucie would have thought. What *would* she have thought? Now that she could see the real Delia, she could no longer remember the one in her head, if there had been one there at all. This one on the picture had straight pale hair—*maybe* it was pale, maybe not; it could have just been faded by the light—and eyes squeezed to slits by the sun. Knees like doorknobs, skinny legs. There was no baby. The picture had been taken some earlier time, in the summer, most likely. It didn't say when.

"Lucie!"

"Yes, Miss Pimm."

"What is that in your lap?"

"Nothing, Miss Pimm."

"It's a photograph, Miss Pimm," Anna said.

"Bring it here, Lucie. Whose picture is this?"

"I don't know, Miss Pimm. I found it in the hall."

"Found articles belong in the Lost Property box, not in your desk."

"I'll take it there, Miss Pimm," Rose Beth offered. "I have to go to the girls' room anyway, and I can drop it off on my way."

But Rose Beth wasn't allowed to go to the Lost Property box *or* the girls' room. It was time to rehearse the class play, and Rose Beth had the biggest part of all, the one where she got to say whole paragraphs of lines. She was a princess and would wear a beautiful costume.

Actually, she didn't get to wear the costume until the end of the play, because she wasn't discovered to be a princess until then; she was thought all along to be a beggar girl, and so she wore ordinary clothes from the hand-me-down box in Mrs. Henderson's room. And the costume she wore at the end wasn't that beautiful either; it was something Miss Pimm had worn long ago, but it was nicer than the hand-me-downs, and anyway, it didn't matter. No one would see the play except for the girls in the lower grades—who else would come?—and they never watched at all. They just played with the auditorium seats, which folded up and down and made slides.

Lucie didn't have a part in the play; she had a responsibility. She worked a pair of ropes so that at the end of every scene, two brown curtains would meet in the middle of a track, and the audience wouldn't see the chairs and tables being rearranged on the stage.

Emily was a village girl in the play, and her lines didn't begin until the third scene. So she was the one Miss Pimm asked to take Lucie's photo to the Lost Property box. And that is why the picture of the four Booths—mother, father, Delia, and Philip—lined up on a front lawn somewhere on the other side of the ocean ended up on Emily's nightstand, and not on Rose Beth's.

CHAPTER TWENTY-FOUR

Lucie's Play

Lucie—the real one—swung the doll's china arms up above its head. The everyday dress peeled off easily and the doll, for a moment, sat naked on the floor. It took a while for the dress-up clothes to be put on, what with the tiny hook and eye on the petticoat. It was a lovely outfit, fashioned from scraps of things found in closets and drawers around Norwood Hall. The pink sash had been pulled from the cuff of Charlotte's sock.

Today, instead of a piano recital, Lucie was going to give a play. She was to be a beautiful princess in a lovely gown. In her play a handsome prince would come to the princess's room and sit on her pillow. "Oh, how dreadful!" she would cry when she saw him. "I don't want a handsome prince at all. Go away!" and she would give him a little slap to send him off. Instantly he would turn into a little green bird, which is what she had wanted all along.

Greenheart was to be the little bird and Emmett was to be the prince. "You get to say you want to marry me, Emmett, and Greenheart will sing a bird song. But I have the biggest part of all. I have more lines than anybody."

Emmett hopped over and put his face close to his sister's and then close to his mother's. "No, you don't," he said. "Mumma has more. Don't you, Mumma? Don't you have more lines than Lucie?" and his hand ran along the cracks on Mumma's china skin.

"Stop that, Emmett," his sister told him. "It's time to put your good clothes on."

Emmett's good clothes were a pair of black felt pants that came down to his shoes and a pale gray shirt made from a corner of a Norwood Hall sheet. The buttons weren't buttons at all. They were a tiny pin. The real Lucie put her fingers on the girl doll's hands and together they fastened it shut.

"And now the play will begin," the girl doll announced to Mumma and Dada sitting side by side, to Olive behind the sofa, and to Mr. Broome at the drawing room door, his eyes like upturned smiles, his smile a half-shut eye.

Lucie spoke her lines with lots of feeling, and Greenheart sang his three high tweets so everyone could hear. Emmett, though, didn't say his lines at all. Instead, he told the audience that he was going to say a poem.

"A poem!" exclaimed Olive. "I love poems. They strengthen the soul."

"It's my pig poem and I made it up all by myself in my own head. Here's how it goes:

> *"What*
> *Would a pig*
> *In an ig-*
> *Loo*
> *Do,*
> *If the ig-*
> *Loo*
> *Came*
> *Un-*
> *Glued?"*

There was more, but Lucie told him to stop, as he was ruining her play.

The real Lucie had decided from the beginning that Emmett would be the silly one. Mumma would be the beautiful one, and the kind one, too. Dada would be the funny one, and Olive would be like whoever Lucie's teacher was, which meant she wouldn't change very much from year to year.

Mr. Broome didn't come along until Lucie found another clothespin on Mrs. Henderson's floor, and she hadn't quite made up her mind what he was like. As for the china Lucie, she would be a great many wonderful things all at once: beautiful and kind and sensible and smart. *Gifted,* in fact.

"That was a lovely poem," Mumma said. She always

said things were lovely, even if they weren't.

"It sounds more like a riddle than a poem," Olive said.

"How can it be a riddle," Emmett replied, "if there's no answer?"

Olive was silent for a long while. "I give up," she finally said. "How?"

"Everybody be *quiet!*" the princess yelled. "The play isn't *over.*"

At the end of the last scene, Greenheart sang his three high notes and there was a lot of applause. Mumma said the costumes were beautiful, and Dada said that Lucie didn't really need a costume to be a princess—she was beautiful just the way she was.

CHAPTER TWENTY-FIVE

The Feather

Miss Pimm took up the book about the Pendletons and their lovely big house on the river. (*"But Mamma,"* Frank *once said, "our house is not on the river; it's next to it. If it were on the river, we should all get wet, shouldn't we?"* and Miss Pimm had reminded everybody that Frank frequently misunderstood English usage. "It adds humor to his character," she explained.)

Today the Pendletons were all getting ready for an adventure at a country fair. They spent a great deal of time packing food into a straw hamper and deciding on the proper clothes to wear. Josie had trouble choosing between a flowered frock and a checkered one, and Mrs. Pendleton kept the others waiting while she tried on first one hat and then another. It was nearly noon before they finally took their places in the pony cart, *"eagerly awaiting their day of excitement and adventure,"* Miss Pimm read.

A pinfeather lay in the bottom of Lucie's desk. She had pulled it by its tail from her pillow that morning and tucked it into the sleeve of her shirt. It flew around among her papers now as she blew little puffs at it through her lips, and now and then it sailed across the moon of light like a lone bird.

"What are you doing, Lucie?"

"Nothing, Miss Pimm."

"Pick your head up and speak clearly. I didn't hear you."

"She said something you're not supposed to say, Miss Pimm," Anna said. "She said a name that Mrs. Henderson gets mad at you for when you say it."

"What was it that you said, Lucie?"

"Nothing, Miss Pimm."

"I heard her say something bad, Miss Pimm, and her desk is full of tissues that she already blew her nose in."

"Close your desk, Lucie."

"Yes, Miss Pimm."

"And watch what you say when you speak to me."

A feather had lain on the sand that day—a large feather, white and long, from a gull most likely, although Lucie had hoped it was a swan's. It was her father who had found it. "Oh, Lucie, look at *this*," he had cried. "It's a mermaid pen. It's how mermaids write to one another. Somewhere nearby there's a message just for you," and he scrabbled about in the sand, his head down low. "Here it is!" he called out at last. "Do you see these tiny words?" He pointed to the claw prints of a crab or a bird. "Can you read what it says?"

"No." She couldn't read what anything said. She hadn't even started school.

"That's because it's written in mermaid. I'll translate it for you. It says, 'Dear Lucie, The next meeting of the mermaid club will be held this Tuesday at daybreak in the exact middle of the ocean. Please come. Bring dues.' Oh, Lucie, how lucky you are. It isn't every mermaid who gets invited to join the mermaid club. And look here. It's written by the mermaid queen herself. She's president of the club. I recognize her hand."

"What's dues?"

"Dues? It's the plural of dew. They want you to bring dew from different things, like spiderwebs and dandelion leaves. Tips of grass, too. Whatever you can find. We'll begin looking tomorrow in the garden."

What garden?

Josie and Frank Pendleton rode on a carousel at the fair that day, and they ate a great number of biscuits. Mr. and Mrs. Pendleton walked about a lot, and Mrs. Pendleton bought each of the children something nice—a toy boat for Frank and a doll's tea set for Josie. *"Josie thanked her mother very prettily,"* Miss Pimm read.

The Adventures of the Pendletons was Miss Pimm's favorite

book. She read it to her class every year. "Why is this a worthy book, class?" she asked.

"Because it teaches us about English clothes from long ago?"

"Because it teaches us about English customs and how they lived?"

"Because it teaches us about English usage?"

"*The Adventures of the Pendletons* is worthy because it teaches us to be respectful of our elders. Notice how politely Josie and Frank thank their mother and father for their gifts."

Later, when Lucie had finally wriggled out of her mermaid tail, she and her father played hangman in the sand, using the feather for a pen. It was early evening by then, and their shadows stretched, long and thin, from the middle of the beach to the edge of the sea. Lucie watched as the waves washed over her distant shadow head, again and again and again.

Her father drew a row of dashes in the sand and a little stick gallows for the man to be hanged. "Guess a letter, Lucie," he had said, and she had guessed "L" for Lucie, hoping he would spell her name. But she was wrong, and he drew a little head below the gallows. "Guess again," but she missed this time, too. The word he had chosen was full of letters she never thought to say, and the man on the gallows grew bigger, piece by piece.

Except it wasn't a man. It was a bird: a wonderful bird with great striped wings and a beak like the blades of a jackknife. "We're playing hangbird, Lucie," he said, and when they finished that word, they played hangcow, and after that hangmouse. At the end, he drew two sets of dashes, and soon Lucie saw her name spelled out at last. She missed only twice, and the figure her father drew on the gallows was a circle on a stick.

"What's that?" she had asked.

"It's a nail."

"A nail?"

"We're playing hangnail now," and he'd laughed, but it was years before Lucie got the joke, and then, of course, it was too late.

The Pendleton family didn't reach home until after sundown. Frank fell asleep with his head in his mother's lap on the ride home, and Josie pretended that her new doll had fallen asleep on *her* lap. There had been no adventure, after all. Just *being* at the fair was the adventure. After supper, they began to play beggar-my-neighbor, but Frank fell asleep again in the middle of the game and had to be carried off to bed.

"And now, Lucie," her father said, just as they were about to leave the beach for the night—for *always*, as it turned out—"you must write a letter back to the mermaids. They're waiting for your reply." He took her hand and walked with her to the very edge of the water, where the sand was hard and smooth. "Now, tell me what to say, and I'll translate it into mermaid for you."

"Tell them I'll be there on Tuesday," she said, as he made little marks like fish scales in the sand. "In the exact middle of the ocean. And tell them that I'm happy, and I want to stay like this forever."

"That's a nice letter, Lucie. And now let's mail it."

"How?"

"Wait and you'll see. In just a moment, a wave will put the letter in its pocket and carry it to the middle of the sea." And that is just what happened. Lucie watched it go.

She smoothed the pinfeather against her thumb over and over until its fine gray lashes stuck together in a fan. Then she slipped it once again inside her sleeve. It would make a nice ornament for Mumma's hat.

CHAPTER TWENTY-SIX

Another Letter from Delia

Dear Lucie,

Guess what. Mr. Huggins banged his head again, and in the same place, too. I don't mean the same place on his head. I mean in the house. Francy says why doesn't he look where he's going, but she should talk.

Lizzie is getting bigger and bigger. She has spots all over her face. Not all over her face, Philip says. Not in the spaces in between. He gets stupider by the day. He calls the baby Busy Lizzie, even though my mother says don't. That's the name of a plant, she says, not a person. Philip says it's from a poem he knows. He didn't tell her what the poem says, but he told me. It says, 'Oh, you put me in a tizzy, busy Lizzie, dizzy Lizzie.' That's the whole thing. It's a horrid poem. He made it up himself. He's been doing that a lot lately, making up poems. They're all horrid. He's going to put them in a book.

Yesterday my father showed me how to draw a face out of numbers. You make a nose from a 6, and the lips are a lying down 8. The ears are 3's. Tell me some things your father does.

This house still seems very strange. There's something in the walls, maybe, that we can't see. Odd things happen. I think someone somewhere is making them happen. This morning I said a word I never heard of before. Chaconne. Francy never heard of it either. Mr. Huggins said it means some kind of music. Why would I want to say that?

My mother says Lizzie's spots are prickly heat, but how can that be possible? It snowed yesterday.

When are you going to write to me?

Do you want to be best friends? I do.

Your friend,
Delia

CHAPTER TWENTY-SEVEN

Olive's Birthday

"Olive," Mumma called, "did you know that today was your birthday?"

"It is?" Olive asked.

"It is?" Emmett cried. "Is that true, Olive? Today's your birthday? Why didn't you say?"

"I clean forgot, Emmett," and because it was her birthday and a special day, Dada didn't say that she also forgot to clean. Instead, he told her to put on her best clothes, which were her satin gloves, and he announced that the rest of the day would be spent playing games.

Lucie—the real one—hopped Olive up the stairs and into her attic room, where she removed from the solid oak wardrobe the two pink strips that were Olive's party clothes and wound them around the loops of her pipe cleaner arms. Then she laid her in the wooden tub, so she could get nice and clean without catching a chill. That gave Lucie a chance to set out the thumbtack and reinforcements in the drawing room so they could play quoits, and to arrange the square snips of paper for their game of cards.

"But what shall we give to Olive for a present?" Emmett asked.

"Bracelets," Lucie said, "made from quoits."

"Then what shall we use for quoits?"

"Olive's bracelets. We can use her arm in the game, and throw the quoits at it, instead of at the spike. That way she won't have to bend down to pick them up." And that was a good idea, since Olive couldn't bend at all.

At first, Olive objected to having her satin-gloved hand used as a ringtoss spike, but Dada said it wasn't ringtoss, it was bracelet-toss. "If it were ringtoss, we would aim for your finger."

"She has no fingers," Mr. Broome reminded everybody. Mr. Broome had been invited to join in the games, and so instead of retiring to the space beneath the stairs where he ordinarily lay from Tuesday to Tuesday, he leaned against the drawing room doorway with the little half smile on his face and his eyes half shut. "Olive has no fingers at all." *Oleeve*, he called her.

"Neither have you, Mr. Broome," Olive said. She was beginning to sound as she did when she grew impatient with the children. "And you call yourself a piano teacher."

Mr. Broome's eyes remained half closed. "I call myself Mr. Broome," he answered. *Meester* Broome.

"Well, I never!" Olive exclaimed. "I never in my whole *life!*"

"Oh, Olive," Mumma said now. "You mustn't quarrel on your birthday. Shake hands with Mr. Broome and let's get on with our game."

"He'll soil my satin gloves," Olive said.

"Glove," Mr. Broome corrected. "I shake only one hand."

Olive grew even angrier and hopped up and down on both feet. "Watch what you say to me!" she cried, but it was Emmett who answered her this time. "How can he, Olive? The words are all invisible when they come out of his mouth."

It was Dada who finally got Olive and Mr. Broome to stop their quarrel so the game could begin, and in just a few minutes, Olive had five white bracelets encircling her pink satin arm.

They played beggar-my-neighbor after that, with the cards the real Lucie had made long before—little faces snipped from her geography book and glued, upside down and downside up, to paper scraps. And then they played donkey, using Mumma's scarf with the holes they could see through. Mr. Broome bumped into things all the same, because he didn't quite understand the rules, and Mumma had to keep moving the baby's cradle out of his way.

Somewhere, far, far away from the Babbidge house, a long bell sounded. Olive moved into the kitchen. "Half past on the dot," she announced, facing the clock with its single downturned hand. "The end of the day!" and then she toppled to the floor.

"Olive's had another spell!" Mumma cried.

"A spill," Emmett said, before Dada had a chance to.

"Spell, Emmett," his sister corrected. It wasn't nice to make fun of Olive on her birthday.

"Spell Emmett?" he asked, and he began to do just that, remembering to say *capital E.*

"Be *still!*" Mumma scolded. "We must all be quiet until Olive comes to."

"Comes to what?"

The distant bell sounded once again: dinnertime at Norwood Hall. The real Lucie leaned back on her heels and swept up the pile of paper snow. Then she put the dolls away one by one: Emmett in his bed for tomorrow's nap; Dada at the side of the house, fifteen doll paces from the front door; Mumma on the sofa, the cradle at her feet; Olive in the kitchen, her head against the icebox; Mr. Broome in his room beneath the stair; and, finally, the china doll Lucie, just outside the front door, where tomorrow after school she would enter once again, crying, "Olive! Olive, Olive, *Olive!* I'm *home!*"

CHAPTER TWENTY-EIGHT

The Grounds

The Grounds were what any other children in any other place would have called the playground: a fenced-in field just outside the back door where, after lunch each day and again at three o'clock, everyone gathered to do what was not allowed inside.

But Norwood Hall hadn't always been what it was now, and it borrowed names for places from uses long past. The large square room beside the entrance hall was the Visitors' Room—although no one ever came to visit—because once long ago Norwood Hall had been what Miss Pimm called a rest asylum: "a place for persons who were neither sick nor well," she told them. "Nobody ever says asylum anymore," she added. "We say *home.*"

And the room in which the younger girls slept was the Pottery, from the days when Norwood Hall had been a place for making things—"neither large nor small," Miss Pimm said. Once, too, Miss Pimm told them, the building had been a department store, but that was hard to believe. What could possibly have been sold here that people couldn't buy close to their homes? Still, the room where Mrs. Henderson slept was called the Trade Room, and the place where they hung their outdoor clothes was the Exchange.

Now, of course, Norwood Hall was what it was—a place for girls who were neither this nor that. Nobody ever said orphans anymore, either.

Even so, other children would have found it hard to call the Grounds a playground, because there was nothing there on which to play. No swing, no slide, no knotted rope slung from a tree. No tree. No painted grids and circles on the ground. Stones, though, and hard clumps of grass that never pulled out and never changed from brown to yellow or green. Also, here and there, a wire basket for trash. Surprises sometimes could be found in these. Crows knew about them and so did Lucie.

"Hey, Goosey-Loosey, what's that in your hand?"

"It's mine."

"I didn't say whose, I said what. Hey, Anna, help me find out what's in Goose's hand."

"I bet it's something stolen."

"I bet it's Rose Beth's hanky."

"Hey, Rose Beth. Goose has your hanky and she won't give it up."

"Hold her hand behind her back."

"It won't go."

"*Make* it go." And Lucie cried out something she had never before spoken aloud, although of course she said it in her head every day.

"MUMmer!" Emily repeated. "What's *that* supposed to mean?"

"It's some crazy language she speaks," Daisy said. "It means something you're not allowed to say."

It was necessary to pull back only two of Lucie's fingers. The others unfolded by themselves.

"It's *candy.*"

"Where'd she get it?"

"Stole it, I bet. From Miss Pimm. Let's tell."

"No, let's eat it."

"But it's *green*. Who would want to eat green candy?"

"No, it's not. That's just the cellophane. Look, it's white underneath."

"Hey, it's mints. White mints."

"Ooh, mints are my favorite. They taste like sparks. Let's everybody have some sparks. Let's see who can keep them on their tongue the longest before they melt. Hey, Claire, look! White mints!"

It was Emily who won. She didn't move her tongue at all, and her mint lay upon it like a thin plastic ring long after everybody else's had dissolved into paste.

"I know how to make a telescope from the box," Charlotte said. "You roll it around like this and then

131

you look through. It makes everything come closer."

"No, it doesn't," Rose Beth said, taking it from Charlotte. "It makes it look the same, except green."

"Punch a hole in it, maybe."

"Take the cellophane off."

Claire finally made it work, or said she did. "See that fence over there? It gets really close when you look with one eye."

"Look at this, Lucie," her father had said late that day, leading her by the hand. They were no longer on the beach, but on a boardwalk lined with—what *were* they, anyway? Not shops. *Places.* With things you could buy. Or eat. Or do. "Look, Lucie." They had entered a place called Fun something. Fun City. Land. Town. And he was steering her toward a—what? A big box, a machine, maybe—a metal case with an opening on top for looking through. "It's a peep show, Lucie," her father had said, and he'd stood her on a block so she could see. "Look inside," and she'd fitted her face into a curved metal frame. Her father dropped a coin into a slot somewhere and suddenly, before her eyes, a man and a lady in clothes of long ago were twirling round and round in what must have been a dance. They smiled into each other's faces, but their words, if they spoke them, made no sound at all. And the music must have played inside their heads, because the room was as quiet as the inside of an egg. Even their feet fell in silence, as though on snow.

Round and round they went, in a red-brown room with windows and a door and candles on the walls. Somewhere in the corner—was she seeing this right?—was a tiger sound asleep, and Lucie caught her breath. But no, it was a blanket of some sort, with stripes, red-brown like the room, like the man, like the lady in his arms.

How did so many things—a whole *room*, with windows and a door and people and all—fit inside a box that she could hold between her hands? "Why do they live in there?" she had asked. "Why?" her father had repeated. "Because it's their house. Everybody has a house, and this is theirs."

And then, smack! everything—room, man, lady, blanket—went black, as though a window blind had suddenly been pulled. Lucie rattled the box to bring it back, but the dark remained in place, and the lady and her partner had vanished altogether, gone away for good, like people in a dream.

"Where'd they go?" she asked.

"They went outside," her father answered.

"Outside?" Lucie searched among the faces of the people on the boardwalk, but none of them belonged to that pair in the room. "Where?"

"Oh, not *our* outside. *Their* outside. Didn't you see

that door in their room? Well, it leads to an outside all their own, with a boardwalk and an ocean and miles and miles of sand. And, Lucie, do you know what they will do? They will walk on the boardwalk until they find a peep show, and they'll put a nickel in and guess what they will see."

"I don't know." Lucie lowered her face once again into the viewer. A beach was in there, behind the dark? An ocean? "How come I can't see the room they were just in?"

"Because they blew out all the candles when they left."

Nothing was left now of the candy except the cellophane wrapper, crackling like a fire as it undid its crumples on the ground. But it was the wrapper, not the candy, that Lucie had wanted all along—the cellophane wrapper, smooth and clear and seaweed green. She pressed out its wrinkles between her tightened knees and tore it very carefully in two.

CHAPTER TWENTY-NINE

Delia's Letter

Dear Lucie,

Francy and Mr. Huggins have just had a terrible row. Nobody knows how it started. They had never quarrelled before, but all of a sudden Francy was yelling her head off, telling Mr. Huggins that he would improve his time if he tidied up his room every day. "Improve your time" is how she talks these days. Like a school-mistress. Then he yelled back that she was a cow. A proper cow, is what he said. Next thing, she was taking her suitcase down from the cupboard. She said she was going to leave if Mr. Huggins stayed another minute. She said our house wasn't big enough for the two of them to live in at the same time. Philip said yes it was, and he began to measure out the rooms with a yardstick, but he was just being stupid, as usual. I do hope she doesn't go. I never thought I cared about her before, but I do. She's like this marble head of Shakespeare we have on our mantelpiece. I don't take much notice of it most of the time, but I would mind awfully if someone took it away.

Is Olive like that? Would you mind awfully if she left? Tell me about her. I don't want Mr. Huggins to go away either. Philip and I would have no one to say nasty things about if he did. Also, he pays ten pounds a fortnight to live here, and my father says without that we would have no sweet for dinner. What does your father do? Mine works at a place where they make spoons, but he doesn't make them himself. He sits at a desk and adds up numbers.

This is my fifth letter to you and you haven't written back once. You must be very busy with your friends. Do you already have a best friend? Could I be your best friend in England? Let me know.

Your friend,
Delia

CHAPTER THIRTY

The Costumes

"Mumma!" This time it wasn't Olive's name that Lucie called when she arrived home after school. It was Mumma's. "Mumma, where are you?" Mumma was where she'd been all day, and all night, too, as it happened—propped on the sofa, with Maud in the cradle at her feet. "Mumma, guess what! I've thought of what you and Dada can be for the masked ball, and I've brought you your costumes as well."

"Lucie, how wonderful! What are we to be?"

"I can't say until Dada comes home, but it's something very lovely."

"Is it goblins, Lucie?" asked Emmett, suddenly appearing from his nap. "Will Mumma and Dada be goblins for the ball? Make them be goblins, Lucie, like the ones that live in the flush thing in the bathroom. I hear them every time someone pulls that string. They scare me when I take my nap. Be goblins, Mumma, and take along the ones upstairs so I won't be scared anymore."

"Emmett, there *are* no goblins in the flush thing,"

Lucie told him. "If there were, they'd drown. There's water up there."

"They're water goblins. I know, because I've seen them. They had bathing suits on."

Olive brought tea just then, so nobody had to answer him, and then at last, Lucie was able to call out, ". . . thirteen, fourteen, fifteen! It's Dada! Guess what, Dada! I've thought up what you and Mumma can be at the masked ball. The ball is tonight, and I've made costumes for you both!"

"Wonderful, Lucie. What are we to be?"

"Well, Mumma is going to be the mermaid queen who lives in the exact middle of the ocean, and you are going to be the mermaid king who lives there, too."

"The mermaid queen!" Mumma cried. "And, Dada, you are to be the king! Remember? The ones who have the club?"

"And collect dues," Dada remembered.

"From spiderwebs and dandelion leaves. Where are the costumes, Lucie?"

"They're here." She brought out the two green cloaks and, with the real Lucie's help, fastened them around her parents' necks.

"Oh, Lucie, how very beautiful they are!" Mumma exclaimed, turning slowly around. "And listen to them crackle! Like a fire. Like a bright green fire."

"Like breaking waves," Dada added. "Like waves making splinters on the sand."

"Green splinters," the china Lucie put in.

"Oh, Lucie, they are beautiful," Mumma said again.

"They're see-through," Emmett observed. "You can see right through them to what's underneath, which is Mumma and Dada."

"And Mumma," the china Lucie said, ignoring her brother, "I've brought you something nice to go with your mermaid gown. It's a feather from a gull and you can wear it in your hair," and with the real Lucie guiding her hand, she taped the little pinfeather to Mumma's head.

"Oh, Lucie," Mumma said. "I must look at myself to see how very beautiful I am," and she stood before the mirror—a smoothed-out strip of foil from a stick of chewing gum.

"You look like a sea goddess," Dada told her. "Like a seabird," Lucie said. Olive said she looked like an ocean queen, and Emmett, still lying on the floor, said she looked like a mackerel. "A nice green mackerel with a feather in its hat."

From somewhere far away came the sudden long bell announcing dinner at Norwood Hall. "Half past on the dot!" Olive cried, without actually consulting the kitchen clock this time.

The real Lucie's legs ached as she unfolded them from their long crouch, and she hobbled to the storeroom door. The second dinner bell sounded, and she quietly turned the knob, when suddenly she thought of something.

Returning to her crouch, she reached into the dollhouse kitchen and lifted Olive from her station beside the icebox. Then she did something she had never done before. Grasping Olive's pipe cleaner arm between her fingers, she gave it a sudden, sharp twist, bending it out of shape and leaving it to dangle like a broken wing. "Ow!" she shrieked in her head for Olive. And although she didn't also shriek "Mrs. Babbidge!" it was Mumma, still wearing her cellophane cloak, who came running in from the hall.

"Oh, Mrs. Babbidge," Lucie cried for Olive, "I've hurt my arm something terrible. I caught it in the icebox door, and now *look* at it!"

"Oh, poor Olive," Mumma said. "Dada, come help me," she called out. "Olive has caught her hand in the icebox door and it's all bent out of shape."

"The icebox door's bent out of shape?" Emmett inquired, coming in from the drawing room.

"No, Emmett, Olive's *arm*. Help me fix her up."

Emmett helped by fetching Mumma's brown scarf, and Dada wound it around and around until Olive's arm couldn't be seen at all. Then Lucie returned all the dolls, with the exception of Olive, to their original posts. Olive was put upstairs in her attic bed—beside the bathtub, the chandelier on the floor, the chair without the seat, and the solid oak wardrobe with her satin gloves and flannels—so she could rest.

CHAPTER THIRTY-ONE

The Frieze

"Lucie's personage has sent her another letter," Miss Pimm remarked, handing Lucie an envelope from Delia. "How many of you continue to receive correspondence from your personages?"

Anna's hand went up. She had gotten a birthday card from her personage, but that was because he was her uncle.

"Put your letter away for now, Lucie," Miss Pimm told her. "You may open it later. Today is a special day."

Today marked the culmination of an important project. Lucie's letter from Delia could wait.

Early in the school year, Miss Pimm had appeared in class with a heavy roll of brown paper under her arm. "We're going to make a freeze today, class," she had said, or seemed to say. "Who can tell us what a freeze is?"

The answer seemed too simple, so no one answered. "Is it the plural of free?" Daisy finally guessed. No, it wasn't. Miss Pimm wrote the word on the board so everyone could see that Anna was wrong. "A frieze," she explained, "is a decorative border, usually on a building." They were going to wrap a paper border around Norwood Hall? "Our frieze is going to be placed high on the walls of our classroom, and it is going to be an *historical* frieze." Miss Pimm always said *an* historical something. "We are going to depict the flow of time from the beginning of recorded history to the present. We are going to make a time line, class, and it will sweep around all four walls of our room."

The scroll of paper was cut into long strips after that and laid across the floor. Each girl was given an epoch to portray. An epoch was not what Rose Beth had said it was, or Anna, either. They had looked up the wrong spelling in the dictionaries in their laps. An epoch was an important period of time. Little by little, with drawings and compositions, the girls would cover the brown paper frieze with events of history, and when it was completed it would stretch all around the room. "Like an ornamental band on a monument, class," Miss Pimm had told them.

Rose Beth and Emily had picked the Dawn of Civilization, and they had painted rows of brown pyramids on a field of yellow sand. Daisy's epoch was the Greeks. She had traced a picture of the Parthenon in a geography book. Charlotte had the Renaissance, and she had pasted a picture postcard of the Mona Lisa on her portion of the frieze. Miss Pimm said it was all right to use postcards, as it would not be fair to an artist to copy his picture. Lucie, Claire, and Jane had the Modern Era. Claire had drawn a picture of an airplane and Jane had made a large cardboard telephone. Lucie had done a gray piece of paper.

"What is this meant to be, Lucie?" Miss Pimm had asked, holding Lucie's picture up so everyone could wonder along with her.

"I don't know, Miss Pimm."

"Pick your head up, Lucie. I can't hear you."

"I don't know, Miss Pimm." Louder this time.

"You don't know what you drew in your own picture? What is all this gray?"

"It's the sky, Miss Pimm."

"The sky?"

"Before the stars come out."

"And how does that fit into the Modern Era?"

"It's a new sky. It's from six years ago, Miss Pimm, in the summer."

Jane had been asked to complete Lucie's picture, and she had added a moon to the sky and a rocket ship with someone in a spacesuit at its side. Then she had pasted it to the end of the brown paper roll.

Today the frieze was all finished, and everyone was to help Miss Pimm tape it to the wall. Miss Pimm didn't need much help with the taping itself. She stood on her desk and positioned the long strips of paper just below the ceiling, as Claire and Jane handed them to her. What she did need help with was moving from epoch to epoch, and Daisy and Anna were appointed to push the desk slowly around the room "in long, slow movements," Miss Pimm instructed them, "so as not to cause any abrupt stops."

"What a splendid accomplishment, class," Miss Pimm announced when, an hour later, the frieze was all in place. It began just above the door with the Dawn of Civilization and traveled around all four walls until it met itself again with the Modern Age. "Time flows," Miss Pimm told them, "uninterrupted," and she walked around the room, letting her yardstick follow the flow of time from century to century.

In fact, though, there were interruptions. The dome of the classroom bell hung like a moon above Daisy's Parthenon, and the round electric clock was a setting sun behind Emily's pyramids. Windows were interruptions, too. In between Anna's picture of the Battle of Hastings and Enid's other picture of the Battle of Hastings was an oblong view of the Grounds, with its bare dirt field, its stones, its wire litter basket, its crows, its clumps of brown grass. And, along the left-hand wall, the wide, wide window—centuries wide—where the bean jungle grew, thick and tangled now and erupting here and there in creamy blooms.

It was that gray hour between day and night when the light has left the sky but the dark and the stars have not yet come to take its place. Lucie and her parents were sitting across from one another on a train. The skin on Lucie's shoulders was beginning now to sting, and she leaned away from the stubble of her seat back. She was riding backward, and the landscape unscrolled outside the window, like the frieze in Miss Pimm's classroom, in disconnected scenes: a farm, a factory, a wall of housefronts, a farm again, a billboard with a cowboy on a horse.

Her father reached into a pocket and pulled out an envelope of sand. "Look what I've brought back from the beach," he had said, sprinkling some grains into the hollow of his hand. "Do you know what these are?"

"They're sand," she had answered. She had seen him collect it as they'd walked away from the ocean at the end of the day. Trudging through the sand was like walking in a dream: No matter how hard she tried, she couldn't make herself go any faster. On and on they had plodded, into the low-lying sun, dragging their long shadows behind them like wet towels. Her father had produced an envelope from somewhere and funneled into it a thin stream of sand.

"Wrong," he was saying now. "They're seeds. Beach-flower seeds. Did you know that? Beachflowers grow from them. Tomorrow we'll plant them in our garden, and water them each day. And then you'll see. In a month, or maybe two, the whole garden will be in bloom." That garden again. Where was it? Lucie could not remember. Just the beach, and the train going home. *What* home?

"Did you see those beautiful beachflowers in the sand today?"

She tried to think. "No."

"Of course you did, Lucie. You couldn't miss them. They bloom early every morning and fold up their petals when the sun goes down. Don't you remember? They've got long stiff stems and huge striped blossoms. So huge, in fact, that people lie beneath them to keep the sun off their backs."

"Oh, umbrellas you mean."

"Beachflowers."

"Lucie's opening her letter, Miss Pimm," Anna said.

"Put your letter on my desk, Lucie," Miss Pimm ordered. She had reached the Renaissance, at the corner of the back wall, and her yardstick was tapping Charlotte's postcard of the Mona Lisa. "The Renaissance was an heroic era," she continued.

*   *   *

Lucie didn't get to open Delia's letter until she was out on the Grounds after lunch. She undid the flap with the tip of her thumb and then quickly ran her eye down the page to see if it said what she expected it to say, and of course it did.

CHAPTER THIRTY-TWO

Another Letter from Delia

Dear Lucie,

Mr. Huggins and Francy still haven't got to be friends, but at least she didn't leave. Maybe when they do become friends, they'll kiss. Do you like romance? I do, awfully. I think about romance all the time. I think about all the romances there had to be just to get me. Here's what: First my mother and father had to have a romance. That's two people. Then their mothers and fathers had to have romances to get them. That's four. Then their mothers and fathers. That's eight. Then theirs and theirs and theirs and theirs, all the way back to when everybody was cavemen. That's millions of romances. And now think of this: If just two of those cavepeople had a row, then the whole thing would have been ruined, and I would never have been born at all. Do you think about things like that? I do. I think about what it would be like if I wasn't born and somebody else was born instead. Except I wouldn't be that somebody else. I wouldn't be anyone at all, ever, in all eternity. What would that be like? I wonder.

Here's what else I wonder: What if all you ever got to be in all eternity was just an insect? I mean, if everybody gets to be only one thing in the whole world ever, what if you had to waste that on being some kind of a beetle? Or a germ. Or one of those flies that live for only one day. I think that would be a terrible thing. Also, what if all you really are is somebody in someone else's dream and when they wake up you'll disappear? What if that? Tell me some things you wonder.

Maybe Francy and Mr. Huggins will have a romance, but who would fancy her? She looks a fright. Especially now. She caught her arm in the fridge door last week and has to carry it about with her day and night all wrapped up like a parcel. Mr. Huggins says she looks as though she's holding a goose.

Your best friend in England,
Delia

PART THREE

CHAPTER THIRTY-THREE

Making Up

The first thing Lucie did was straighten Olive's arm. The next was get Olive and Mr. Broome to make up. That took longer. They were gathered, all of them— Olive, Mr. Broome, and the two doll children—in the kitchen, where Mr. Broome didn't even belong. He didn't belong in the dining room either. He was not a conventional lodger, like Mr. Huggins, who took his evening meals with the family. Mr. Broome didn't take any meals at all. "Where would he take them?" Emmett once asked. "He has no place to go." Mr. Broome usually spent his entire week, from piano lesson to piano lesson, in the little wedge of space beneath the stairs. But Lucie—the real one—had brought him to the kitchen, and here he was, on a day that wasn't even Tuesday.

"That's an heroic flower you're wearing today, Olive," Lucie made him say. He was the first member of the Babbidge household to comment on the violet taped to Olive's cap.

Olive made no reply, and Mr. Broome repeated what he had said, louder this time.

"Thank you," Olive finally mumbled, although she didn't turn around. Those were the first words they had exchanged since their quarrel on Olive's birthday.

"There's no need to thank him, Olive," Emmett pointed out. "He didn't say *you* were heroic. Just the flower. And you didn't even grow it," which was true. Nobody had grown it. The real Lucie had twisted it into shape from a scrap of paper in the trash bin on the Grounds, which is where she'd found the paper for the china Lucie's poppy.

It was the china Lucie who said that she and Emmett should go into the drawing room, and it was also her idea to leave Mr. Broome and Olive together in the kitchen.

"Olive is entertaining a guest, Mumma," she explained, as she settled on the sofa.

"He didn't look especially entertained," Emmett commented. "He looked bored. His eyes were closed, and anyway, Mumma, what is he doing here at all? It's Thursday."

"He's not here for a lesson, Emmett," Mumma explained. "He's come to see Olive. He's paying a call."

"How much is he paying it?" Emmett asked, but just then Olive appeared at the doorway. "What will you have for tea, Madam?" she asked, as though Mr.

Broome weren't in the kitchen at all. As though he hadn't tried to make up with her by saying something nice about the flower in her hair. As though she didn't have a flower in her hair in the first place. "There are ginger cookies and that's all."

"Then why did you ask what we'd have?" Emmett wanted to know.

Mumma didn't give Olive a chance to reply. "We'll have the ginger cookies," she said, as though there were a choice. "Put them on the—"

The noise outside the storeroom was sudden, loud, and impossible to identify. Lucie—the real one now—jumped up from her cramped position, catching the corner of the dollhouse on her hip and making it rumble. "Shhh," she whispered to the tea table sliding across the rug, to the tiny tea things clattering on their tray, to the churn tipping over in the kitchen, to Mr. Broome and Olive, who were *both* toppling to the floor. "Shhh!" and she threw the green sweater over the roof, as though to silence a caged bird.

What *was* it? First a roar of some sort and then a kind of crash. Voices now. She pulled the ceiling string and darkened the room.

"Hey, it's scary down here."

A scream.

"What happened?"

"I think I stepped on something dead."

"Did it squash?"

"No, it crackled, sort of."

"A rat, probably. That was its bones."

"I think it's stuck to my shoe."

Another scream. "Scrape it *off!*"

"I *can't*. It's *attached*."

"Well, take your *shoe* off."

"NO! Then I'll step on something else with my bare *socks!*"

"Oh, Daisy, feel this wall. It's got goo on it."

"No, slime. I bet there's bats down here. Bats make this stuff that's all slime, and they put it on walls and things. I read that."

"Hey, what's *this*? It's a doorknob or something. Hey, there's a door here."

Lucie turned to stone on the other side of the wall.

"Let's go in. Rose Beth, turn the knob."

"No, you."

"You found it first."

"You thought it up."

"Yeah, but you're closer."

"You thought up coming down here in the first place."

"Let's save it for when we come back." That was Anna.

"I'm not coming back."

"I am." Claire, probably. She always sounded like

that—as though she were about to hiccup. "I like it here. I like slime. I like to scrape it with my fingernails."

"Then you open the door."

Lucie cupped her hand against her nose, so that the sound of her breath would collect in her palm, and not float about in the air around the room.

"No, I'm saving it for next time. This time I want to concentrate on the slime."

"I bet there's somebody living down here."

"Who?"

"A lunatic or something. That's what lunatics do. They live in places like this, with bat slime and all, and dead rats on the floor. I bet that's what's behind the door. A lunatic."

"I bet that's what makes all the slime on the walls."

"Hey, yeah, that's lunatic slime."

"I bet that's what's stuck to my shoe. Lunatic bones."

"Let's get out of here."

And they were gone. Lucie waited a long while after the last of the voices was heard before turning the knob on the door and slipping through the narrow passageway to the stairs. It wasn't until that night that she remembered her sweater.

CHAPTER THIRTY-FOUR

The Earthquake

"Lucie," Miss Pimm said, handing over another letter, "your personage is writing you with unusual frequency. I hope there is nothing unwholesome about this correspondence."

"No, Miss Pimm."

"What does she write about in all these letters?"

"Her career, Miss Pimm. In interior design."

Dear Lucie,

Another odd thing happened yesterday, but this was the oddest of all. We had an earthquake. *Here's how it happened: We were just about to have tea, when suddenly the whole house began to shake, just like that, and everything inside started bouncing around. The tea table ended up in the middle of the sitting room, and all Philip's toys came crashing down the stairs. Also, some dishes broke. Francy and Mr. Huggins were both knocked off their feet and a picture came off its hook. Then, right after that, everything grew dark as night. Philip said it was someone landing from somewhere, maybe. That made Francy scream. It was all dreadful.*

But then, here comes the really odd part. We all ran outside
and, do you know? the sun was shining perfectly well, and nobody
else had noticed a thing. Mr. Gregory who lives next door was
snipping something in his garden, and Tabitha, who lives next
next door, was riding her tricycle up and down the pavement.
The police said it was the smallest earthquake they had ever seen,
but then they'd never seen any earthquake at all. Not even this
one. Oh, and do you know what else? I think Francy and Mr.
Huggins are almost friends again. Just before the earthquake, he
said that she was not quite so clumsy as she used to be, and she
thanked him, although not at all properly. After that they both
fell down.

Sometimes I wonder if you get my letters at all.

Your very best friend of all,
Delia

CHAPTER THIRTY-FIVE

Olive and Mr. Broome Together

"Olive!" Lucie cried. "Olive, Olive, *Olive!*" but no small figure in apron and cap awaited her in the front hall. "Where's Olive?" Lucie asked, as Emmett appeared at the top of the stairs.

"She's in the kitchen." He was at the bottom of the stairs now.

"Well, why isn't she *here?*"

"Because then she couldn't be in the kitchen, which is where she is." Emmett hopped into the drawing room, which was all straightened up, with the tea table back in place and the cups set to rights on their tray.

"What is she doing there?"

"I don't know. Ask Mr. Broome."

"Mr. Broome! Where is he?"

"In the kitchen, too."

Lucie marched into the dining room and stood just outside the kitchen door. There were Mr. Broome and Olive, facing one another across the room—Mr.

Broome leaning against the wall, Olive against the ice-box.

Mr. Broome had a book of some sort tucked into his arm. "I will teach you how to play the piano," he said. *Weel titch.*

"But I have no fingers," Olive protested. "You told me that yourself."

"You don't need fingers," and here Mr. Broome showed Olive his book. *Piano Music for Four Hands*, it said. The real Lucie had printed the words on a scrap of paper torn from her classroom notebook. She had even drawn some music inside—tiny blacked-in circles with short straight stems, some with little tails. "It's hands they want," he explained, "not fingers, and we need four of them." He touched Olive's looped hands with his own. "Two of mine and two of yours."

"Nonsense," Olive said, with what seemed to be a sniff.

"It is not nonsense. Two and two are four, yes?"

"It is impossible for either one of us to play the piano, Mr. Broome, as I am unable to sit down and so are you." She moved quickly about the room and said nothing further.

Mr. Broome also said nothing further, at least for a while, but then he moved forward from the wall and approached Olive. "We will play standing up," he suggested. "It is a sign of laziness to play the piano sitting down. Will you let me give you lessons if we stand up?"

"I'll give it some thought," Olive answered, without turning around. "But I don't think it will do. How would we ever bow when people clapped?"

CHAPTER THIRTY-SIX

The Mammal

Dear Lucie,

Do you know what I think? I think Mr. Huggins is in love with Francy. Can you imagine that? Just a month ago, he said she was a cow, and today when they were in the kitchen I saw him touch her hand. Maybe when he said that about the cow he meant to be nice. Some people like cows. I do, but not to marry. Do you think Mr. Huggins will ask Francy to marry him? I hope so. Then I can get to be bridesmaid at their wedding and wear a flouncy dress. Do you like flouncy clothes? Tell me your favourite colors. Mine are lavender and black. Also, apricot for underwear. If I get to be bridesmaid, that's what I'll wear. The thing I like most about lavender is how it sounds when you say it. What words do you like? Columbine and willow are my other favourites. Philip's is bilge. When he says it, spit comes to the sides of his mouth.

I wish you would write me. I like to imagine where you are, in your big house with all those things in it. Are you rich? Is *that why you don't write? I know three rich people. Please let me know if you're rich, too, so I can make it four. I keep a list.*

Love,
Delia

"Put your letter away, Lucie."

"Yes, Miss Pimm."

"I want all eyes up front." She held up a parcel with punctures in its sides and strange noises coming from within. She spoke sternly. "A very special item has arrived in the mail," she said, "but I will not unwrap it until there is total silence in the room."

"What is it?" Rose Beth called out.

"Is it something alive?" Anna asked.

"I bet it's bugs."

"Ooh, bugs," Rose Beth said.

"Total silence," Miss Pimm repeated.

"Is it okay if we breathe?" Anna asked.

Miss Pimm peeled away the wrapping paper little by little, as though she were undressing a doll, and everyone but Lucie leaned forward. "Total silence. What I am about to reveal becomes agitated at the slightest noise."

"It *is* alive!" Anna shouted. "Just like I said!"

"It's bugs!"

"Spiders!"

"Worms, I bet."

"Be *quiet!*" Rose Beth shouted from across the room.

Miss Pimm put the half-opened package on her desk and stood still as a pillar until everyone was quiet once again. "Severe agitation can cause immediate death in some species," she warned, "especially in the very young."

"It's a baby," Anna whispered. "A bug baby."

Pretty soon all the layers of paper were removed, and Miss Pimm held up for everyone to see a small wire cage enclosing something covered with fur— black, white, and gray.

"It's a PET!" Emily cried, and Lucie watched as, in the next instant, everyone crowded around Miss Pimm's desk, a thing they were never allowed to do.

"Can I pet it?" Claire demanded.

"Can I, too?"

"I said it first."

"Then we can take turns."

"Me, too."

"Stop *pushing.*"

"Can we take it to our room at night, Miss Pimm?"

"Can it sleep with me in my bed?"

"Ooh, look at its nose, how pink."

"Look, it's looking at me. Hey, it likes me! Hey, animal, say hello."

"What is it, anyway?"

"A guinea pig."

"A hamster."

"No, a gerbil."

"A rat."

"Hey, rat, say hello."

"Let's name it."

"How about Blackie?"

"No, Whitey."

"No, Grayey."

"No, Sam."

"No, Ham, for hamster."

"No, Pork."

"No, Bacon."

"No, Swine," said Claire. "Hey, Swine, say hello."

"Sit DOWN!" Miss Pimm's words rose above everyone else's in a voice that was not like her own. "Sit down at *once!*" Lucie was already in her seat, as she had never left it, but Miss Pimm didn't use her as an example. "Return to your seats *immediately!*" she cried out instead, and little by little the room grew quiet.

"The animal in the cage is not a pet," Miss Pimm announced. "It is the subject of our next unit of study. Class, we are about to examine the habits and behavior of a mammal. Who will tell us what a mammal is?"

Claire said it could be a hamster or an elephant, and Daisy said it could be any animal, and Enid said it could be any animal so long as it had four legs, but then Jane asked, Well, what about humans? So Enid said, Well, any animal with arms *or* legs, so long as they added up to four, but then Anna said, Yes, but how about whales? "Whales are mammals," she reminded everybody, "and they're not animals at all; they don't even *have* arms and legs, just little flippers," and Charlotte said, No, that was seals, with flippers. "Maybe their flippers add up to four," Enid suggested.

"A mammal," Miss Pimm began, but she soon stopped. "Lucie, what are you doing in your desk?"

"Nothing, Miss Pimm."

"She's drawing lines on her fingers with marking pen, Miss Pimm," Anna told her.

"Fold your hands on top of your desk, Lucie, and look at me. A mammal," she resumed, "is an animal that nourishes its young with milk."

Her father had nourished *her* with milk, that evening on the train, but he didn't call it milk and he certainly didn't say he was nourishing her. "This is what mermaids drink," he had said, leaning toward her with a small wax carton and a straw. "Can you guess what it is?" and Lucie had known enough to say no. "It's fresh-squeezed shell, that's what, and do you know how it is made? I will tell you. Someone takes a nice fresh shell and squeezes it. Pretty soon, little drops of shell juice come out, and they are collected in containers just like this. Early every morning someone else leaves a container at the door of every mermaid in the sea. Every merman, too. They drink it all day long, sipping it through straws of grass-green glass, and they feed it to their young. All little merbabies are fed on the juice of fresh-squeezed shells. Here, have some," and Lucie had sucked into her mouth a long, slender stream— cold and white and tasting just a little of the sea.

And now Miss Pimm was coming around the room with the hamster—it was a hamster, after all; Rose Beth had been right—and allowing each girl to stroke its coat. "One stroke apiece," she cautioned. "Young animals should not be overhandled." Claire ran only one finger along the hamster's spine, but Daisy used all five. Charlotte used her nail and left a line.

"What are some features of the hamster's coat," Miss Pimm asked as she traveled up the aisle, "that offer protection?"

"It's furry," Enid said, "so you can put it next to you and it makes you warm."

"It's short all the time," Rose Beth said, "so it doesn't have to be cut or anything."

"It's the same colors as the newspaper in its cage, so it can hide in there."

Miss Pimm was at Lucie's desk now and she held out her hand with its single, quivering passenger. "Examine its coat, Lucie, with your eyes, and then stroke it with your hand, but only once."

Lucie gazed into Miss Pimm's palm. It wasn't a coat at all that the animal had on, but a little fur suit cut exactly to size, with sleeves that came all the way down to the toes, and special little slits for the ears to poke through. She put her hand out so she could smooth out its fur.

"What is that all over your *fingers*?" Miss Pimm cried out while Lucie's hand was in midair. "What *is* that?"

"It's marking pen, Miss Pimm," Anna reminded her. "She drew on her fingers in green."

"We don't handle animals with soiled hands," Miss Pimm told Lucie, and she moved on to the desk ahead, which was Emily's.

CHAPTER THIRTY-SEVEN

Olive's Announcement

Lucie went straight up to her room when she came home from school and addressed her pet bird. "Greenheart," she said, "it's me. Lucie," and Greenheart responded with his three clear notes: *Tweet, tweet, tweet,* he sang. One, five, eight, on the scale the real Lucie had learned in music class at school. "Come with me, Greenheart," she said, and with the real Lucie's help, she lifted him from his cage. "Come into the drawing room and sing me a song." She took him between her two china hands and carried him down the stairs.

No one had come into the drawing room yet. Mumma was upstairs with Maud, Emmett hadn't gotten up from his nap, Olive was in the kitchen, and Mr. Broome was in the kitchen with Olive. Dada was still at work. Lucie sat down on the sofa and laid Greenheart on her lap. "There, now," she said. "Let me straighten out your plumes so you'll look nice and smooth." She ran her hand along the fuzz of his small green form. Over and over, she stroked his head, his back, his tail, with the lightest touch ever, so as not to make dents.

"Now, sing to me, Greenheart," she said, and Green-heart did. *Tweet, tweet, tweet*, he sang: one, five, eight; eight, five, one.

"Say you like me, Greenheart," she said after a while. "Say you think I'm nice," and Greenheart did, in the way he knew best.

Greenheart remained on Lucie's lap for a long while, and he lay there still, round and green in the folds of her skirt, when everyone came down for tea.

"Tell me what you did in school today, Lucie," Mumma said, settling next to Lucie and the bird. Maud lay in the cradle at her feet.

"A mammal came in the mail, Mumma, and we all petted it. It liked me best."

"What mammal was it, Lucie?"

"You'll have to guess."

"I know what a mammal is," Emmett said. "It's a mouse and a camel mixed together. I've seen pictures. It looks like a mouse, but it has two humps on its back."

"That's not what a mammal is," Lucie told him. "A mammal is something that nourishes its young with milk."

"Well," he answered, "that's what the mammal in my picture book did, too. It gave its babies milk every day in a little glass. It looked like ordinary mouse milk, but it had two humps in it."

"Oh, Lucie, now I can guess," Mumma said, pretending as usual that she hadn't heard Emmett. "It was a mermaid!" and she gave the cradle a little tilt with her foot. "Mermaids nourish their young with milk, don't they?"

"Yes, Mumma, but they call it shell juice, remember? That's what Dada always says."

"And is that what came in the mail?" Emmett asked. "A mermaid?" But there was no chance to reply, because just then Olive appeared with the tea things.

Mumma moved the cups around on the table with the edge of her china hand, and Emmett bent forward at the waist to help himself to a flat biscuit. Olive remained where she was.

"That will be all, Olive," Mumma said, but Olive didn't move.

Lucie held a bit of lemon biscuit to Greenheart's beak, and he thanked her in three sharp syllables. Emmett lay on the rug with a teacup on his chest, and Mumma stirred and stirred her tea with a spoon. Nobody paid any attention to Olive, who remained where she was, propped between the tea table and the sofa.

"What is it, Olive?" Mumma finally asked.

"Oh, Madam," Olive replied. "I've an announcement to make."

"Oh, lovely, Olive," Emmett said. He propped his head against Maud's cradle. "Say it from the piano, like a poem."

Olive *did* walk to the piano, and she rested a hand on the keys, but she didn't deliver her words as a poem. "My announcement is," she said, "that I am going to be married to Mr. Broome."

CHAPTER THIRTY-EIGHT

Francy's Wedding

Three weeks went by before Delia's next letter came, but of course Lucie knew what it would be about.

Dear Lucie,

Everything turned out as I had dreamed! Mr. Huggins asked Francy to marry him and she said yes and they were married right here in our house. It was a very strange wedding, but it seemed to be what they both wanted. Mr. Huggins wore his everyday clothes, but he found a tall black hat somewhere and put it on his head. Philip said he looked like a marking pen. My mother tried to stop him saying stupid things, as it was a solemn occasion, but he said them anyway. Francy wore a long white veil that she made herself out of something she'd been saving. It looked like a curtain, but my mother said it was perfectly elegant. (She says everything is elegant.) The veil came down to Francy's feet, and Philip had to hold one end when she walked down the stairs, so she wouldn't trip.

He was the ring bearer. He kept saying he wouldn't be, and when my mother asked why not, he said, "Because I can't bear rings," which was supposed to be funny. Nobody laughed, as it was a solemn occasion, but he said it over and over anyway, in case somebody changed their mind. Does your brother say stupid things?

Best of all, I got to be bridesmaid, just as I'd always dreamed, except I didn't get to wear lavender and black with apricot underwear. My mother found a pink dress for me in a shop. It's very old, and my mother said somebody made it by hand. It has a petticoat with a little hook and eye to do up, and there's a pink sash that ties in the back. I carried violets and pink carnations.

My father was best man, and my mother was matron of honor. Philip said Francy should have married my father, because if he was the best man then Mr. Huggins was the worst, but my mother told him to be still. Then came the ceremony, and do you know what? No one had thought to call in the vicar, so they had to marry themselves. They said "I thee wed" to each other and put on their rings and then they kissed. It was an exceptionally ardent kiss, and Mr. Huggins's hat fell off.

It was a lovely wedding, and now it's all over and everything is the same, except we must call Francy Mrs. Huggins and I keep forgetting.

Lots of love from your best friend in England,
Delia

CHAPTER THIRTY-NINE

Forfeits

Sometimes it would happen in December, sometimes not until June. There was no telling. Still, it happened every year: From somewhere on the Grounds, and it could be anywhere—near the school's back door, in the angle where one fence wall met another, in the very dead center of the field—someone, and it could be anyone, would let out a sudden cry: *"Forfeits!"* The sound, raucous as the call of a crow, would freeze for a moment in the air. Everyone on the field would freeze, too. *"FORFEITS!"* And, as with the call of a crow, answers would come, from here, from there. "Forfeits!" "Forfeits!" "Forfeits!" "Choose up teams!"

The first time Lucie had heard that cry, years ago, she had stood stone still and then run back and forth across the field, screaming and looking past her shoulder. "Hey, look at Goose!" someone had shouted. "She thinks the races have already begun. Hey, slow down, Goose. No fair getting a head start." What she had actually thought, though, was that forfeits were something alive and that they were already at her heels.

Now, though, when she heard that call—and it was Charlotte this year who began it—she didn't even bother to look up. There was no need. The teams were picked with great care, and she was never chosen to be on either one.

The forfeit that first year was to climb on the roof, and Lucie had stood apart from everyone else, watching as a row of distant girls picked their way like silent witches across the highest ridge of Norwood Hall.

Except for the people on the teams, no one knew, until the forfeit was carried out, just what it actually would be. The winning team thought it up in secret and the losing team, once told, kept silent, too. It wasn't until the losers would appear, single file along the roof, or stretched out hand to hand on the second-story ledge, that the rest of the school would learn how they would pay. "Somebody died once doing forfeits," Anna said now, and Emily, who was new to Norwood Hall this year, swallowed a mouthful of air.

The games, though, were the same from year to year, and they followed the same order: foot races first, prisoner's base next, crows and cranes last of all.

Daisy was captain of one team this year, Charlotte of the other. They stood side by side and studied the faces of the girls clustered around them. "Jane," Charlotte said, choosing, and Jane detached herself from the group and stood behind her captain. "Anna," Daisy called after a while. "No, Claire," and Claire, not Anna, took her place behind Daisy. Anna was finally picked by Charlotte, and that was just as well, she said, as she knew somewhere inside her that Daisy's team would lose. Losing, not winning, was what mattered in forfeits.

"Call to order!" Charlotte cried when the teams were formed, eight to a side, and they arranged themselves in parallel files. "Foot races first. *Begin!*"

Daisy's team won three of the four foot races—forward, backward, and hopping-left-foot—but Charlotte's team won prisoner's base. So everything rested with crows and cranes, and the girls scattered across the field.

Emily had trouble with the rules. "What am I supposed to *be?*" she kept asking, studying the scrap of paper in her hand. "Whatever your number says," Charlotte explained, or tried to. The rules had been made up at Norwood Hall long ago, no one knew when. "Odds are crows, evens are cranes."

"Well, then, how is anyone supposed to know?" Emily persisted. "They're not," Charlotte replied. "That's the point of the game." That *was* the point of the game: No one was to know who was crane and who was crow; who was captor, who was prey. Not until a right match was made—crow and crane—did one team win a point, the other team lose.

"But what am I supposed to *do*?" Emily kept wanting to know, and she hopped impatiently about on one foot. "That depends on what you are," she was told. "If you're crow, you attack; if you're crane, you escape. But don't let anyone know what you are doing. Just look like you're running around," and that is what Emily did, so that no one knew until she was dragged across the field by Rose Beth that it was crane she had picked. It was a game that was played only once a year, when forfeits was declared.

Whatever it was inside Anna that told her Daisy's team would lose, it turned out, was wrong. Daisy and her winning teammates marched across the field and collected in a tight circle beside the fence while Charlotte's team, in no circle at all, but staying close together all the same, watched.

They had less than two minutes to wait. Daisy herself carried the message across the field. Emily was the only one on Charlotte's team to speak when the orders were delivered. "That's not *fair!*" she cried, but the others hushed her up. Silence was the custom when forfeits were announced at Norwood Hall.

CHAPTER FORTY

Olive's Wedding

"Yes, Mumma, I did," Lucie said. "I had a lovely time in school today. There were relay races, and I got picked first to be on a team. I'm the fastest runner in my class, and hopper, too. I won both the hopping-right-foot race and the hopping-left-foot race."

"I can do better than that," Emmett said, entering from the hallway. "I can hop on both feet at the same time. Do you want to see?"

"No," Lucie answered, but he showed her anyway.

"That's stupid, Emmett," Lucie said. "You're supposed to jump on just one foot when you hop."

"Oh, I can do that, too," and with both feet he landed on Lucie's shoe.

"Mumma! Tell him to *stop* that! He's being stupid on *purpose!*"

"Nobody's stupid on purpose," Emmett answered. "You're stupid because you can't help it, isn't that right, Olive?"

Olive was just bringing in the tea tray. "Isn't it?" Emmett insisted. "Olive?" But Olive didn't reply. "I mean Mrs. Broome," he said. Nobody remembered to call her that, least of all Emmett, even though she'd been married for more than three weeks now. "Aren't you stupid because you can't help it, Mrs. Broome?" But she didn't answer this time either.

"You insulted Olive," Lucie told him.

"No, I didn't. I insulted Mrs. Broome."

There was no excuse for forgetting Olive's new name. Her wedding ring was in plain view on a string around her neck, and her wedding bouquet stood conspicuously in the little round pot on the dining room table. Mr. Broome was conspicuous, too. He stood at her side at all times, with a ring hanging from *his* neck. Right now he was helping arrange the ginger cookies on their plate.

That had all been agreed upon at the wedding: Mr. Broome would help Olive in the kitchen and Olive would help him with the piano lessons. Mostly, that meant leaning against the sofa and listening as Lucie and Emmett played their pieces. "But that's what she always did," Emmett had protested, just as the ceremony was about to begin. "Yes," Mumma agreed, "but now Olive will say if you've struck a wrong note."

"That's no help at all," Emmett went on. "Once I've struck it, it's *struck*, and it's too late to do anything about it."

But "Hold your tongue" was all Mumma answered.

The wedding ceremony was about to begin, and Emmett was to take up his position on the stairs with the bride and groom. "Bride and Broome," Dada had said, but Mumma told him to hold his tongue, too. This was a solemn occasion. It was Olive's only wedding, and everything had to be just right.

Which it was. At first everyone wanted to be in the procession but Mumma pointed out that in that case no one would be in the audience, so she and Dada waited below while the two children attended the couple on the stairs—Lucie in front with the flower petals, Emmett behind with the rings.

Olive looked quite lovely in a long white veil over her black dress, and Mr. Broome looked lovely, too. He didn't wear anything new (he didn't have to; his everyday suit was the right shade of black and his hat was just right, too, or nearly so), but he had a tiny flower in his lapel—or what would have been his lapel if he'd had that kind of jacket.

The layers on the cake held together perfectly well, and nobody tripped on the stairs. Everyone was beautifully behaved, even Emmett, who *could* have said something stupid when Mumma said "Hold your tongue," but who didn't, even though everyone waited for him to do so. Even when Mr. Broome's hat fell off during the kiss, nobody said a word.

"Let's have a race of our own," Emmett suggested now, "right here in the drawing room when we're done with our tea. Everybody can be in it, even Maud. Even Greenheart. We can hop or jump or run or whatever we like. Even sleep, if it's Maud, or sing, if it's Greenheart, and whoever does it the fastest wins."

"I'll skate," Olive said. "I'll skate back and forth along the hall."

"Oh, no," Mr. Broome cautioned her quickly. "You'll slip." *Sleep*, he said.

And then Emmett said, "Well, then Maud will win, because she sleeps fastest of all. See? She's fast asleep already."

"WHAT IF IT'S LOCKED?"

"TRY IT AND SEE."

"NO, YOU."

But these words were spoken by no one in the Babbidge house, and Lucie—the real one—scrambled to her feet and yanked off the light.

CHAPTER FORTY-ONE

The Invasion

"You try it."

"No, you."

"You're the biggest, Jane."

"You're the one who made us lose, Emily. You told what you were in crows and cranes."

"I did not."

"You did so. You kept running around on one foot, like a crane."

"I did not."

"Yes, you did. I saw you."

"I did not. And anyway, *you're* the one who made us lose left-foot-hopping. You skipped instead of hopped."

"Hurry *up!*" But Claire was from the winning team. What was *she* doing out there? Inspecting, most likely. To make sure. Most years they didn't need an inspector. Most years the forfeits were carried out in the open, where everyone, even the teachers sometimes, could see. Last year, though, when Jane's team had to do some terrible thing—Lucie never found out what—in Mrs. Henderson's room, there was an inspector. It was Enid, and she was the one who got caught, too, although she was the only one who hadn't entered the room.

"I'll turn the handle to see if it's locked, but I won't open the door," Lucie heard now.

There was a silence then, and, from the other side of the door, Lucie could see the knob turn slowly to the left.

Another silence, and then, "Okay, so who's going to go in first?"

"Let's all go first together." Anna was whispering. They all were whispering.

"We won't fit."

"I just heard a noise in there."

"Me, too. Somebody's in there."

"The lunatic."

"I'm leaving." Emily again.

"You can't. It's against the rules."

"I don't care. They're just your rules, not real rules."

"You'll die if you don't do forfeits."

"Somebody died when they did do forfeits," Emily answered. "Anna said."

"I just heard something again."

"Maybe it's an animal. That's escaped from the zoo or something. I knew a lion once who got out of his cage and he went into somebody's house."

"That's not true."

"It is so."

"Then how did he get in?"

"He ate the door."

"This door's still here, and anyway, there's no zoos around here."

"Then it's rats. There's rats in there. I can tell by the sound. Scratching, like."

"Jesus Christ." Emily again.

A silence. Then, "You're not supposed to say that."

"Say what?"

"What you just said."

"About the rats?"

"No, after that."

"Jesus Christ?"

"Yeah. You're not supposed to say that. Mrs. Henderson gets mad."

"Well, then, how come Jesus's mother named him that if it's not a nice thing to say?" Emily wanted to know. "How come that?"

Charlotte didn't know, but Claire didn't give her a chance to say so. "Go *in!*" Her voice was no longer a whisper.

"Maybe we should bang on the door a lot, so whatever's in there will get scared away."

"Okay, everybody bang."

"But what if it's a lunatic? He won't have anyplace to go except out here."

Finally, "I don't hear anything anymore."

"Then go in now," Claire ordered.

"How long do we have to stay?" Emily's voice was the easiest to pick out. It shook the most.

"Until I say to come out."

"How long's that?"

"I don't know. Whatever I decide. An hour, maybe."

"But that's not *fair*. What if we get bitten or something?"

"You still have to stay."

"What if we die? People die if rats bite them."

"That's snakes."

"Rats, too. I know someone who died once from rats."

"Who?"

"Someone."

"What if it's snakes in there?" Enid hadn't spoken before. "Snakes live in cellars a lot. Sometimes there are millions of snakes in one room and you don't even know it until they bite you. You think it's a rug or something on the floor."

"It's not snakes. It's a lunatic."

But Claire interrupted them all. "Hurry *up!*" she commanded. "You have to go in by the time I count three," and from inside the storeroom, Lucie saw a thin strip of light spring up at the edge of the door.

CHAPTER FORTY-TWO

Inside the Storeroom

"I can't see."

"Me neither."

"You will in a minute. There's some light from the window."

"That's how he gets in and out, I bet. Through the window."

"Who?"

"The lunatic."

"There's nothing here. It's just an empty room."

"What's this box on the floor?"

"Don't touch it! It's got something on top of it."

"What?"

"I can't see. A sweater or something. Somebody's old sweater."

"The lunatic's."

"What's that thing under it?"

"A box. No. *Hey!* Hey, look at *that!*"

"What?"

"It's a *house*. A *doll*house."

"Hey, let me see."

"Get out of the way, Emily. You're the one who didn't want to come in here, remember?"

"Well, stop pushing, anyway. You didn't want to come in either. You said. What's this? Hey, look, it's got a chimney."

"And it's full of furniture and everything. Look, it's got an upstairs, with beds and all."

"And a tub! Look up here! There's a tub like they used to have. With feet."

"And here's a toilet. With a cord you pull."

"Stop *pushing*."

"Well, I got here first. Look, there's *dolls*. Look at this one, with the dress and everything."

"There's a boy one, too. With pants, sort of."

"Let's play. Let's put the doll on the toilet."

"No, wait. What's this?"

"It's just a clothespin."

"Yeah, but it's got all this black paper stuck to it, and a face, like."

"Here's another one. With a thimble on top."

"For a hat. Hey, what's this walnut shell doing in here, with something white inside?"

"It's what he eats."

"Who?"

"The lunatic."

"There's mostly junk in here. Here's a bunch of re-inforcements and a thumbtack."

"Yeah, well, let's play anyway. I get this doll."

"I get this one."

"No, *I* get that one. I found it first."

"Well, I get this one, then. Anyway, this is better. It's bigger and it's got this shiny dress on, pink. Who wants the other one? It's supposed to be a man, with the long pants."

"I'll take it."

"Claire, you're not even supposed to be in here. You're supposed to be the inspector. You have to stay outside."

"I can do whatever I want. Anyway, you're not supposed to have a good time when you're doing forfeits. You're supposed to suffer."

"We are suffering. It's scary down here."

"Well, I'm going to make you suffer more. I'm going to play with that doll with the dress."

"No, you're not. I had it first. And besides, you're not even supposed to be *doing* forfeits."

"I'm not doing forfeits. I'm making you suffer, by playing with the doll. So give it over."

"No."

"Yes."

"No. Hey, look *out.*"

"I said give it to me."

"Well, stop grabbing. You're *breaking* it."

A scream.

Silence.

"Who screamed?"

"I don't know."

"Let's get out of here. There's somebody in here."

"*Who?*"

"The lunatic!"

"Take the dolls and let's run."

CHAPTER FORTY-THREE

Sick

Who was that a picture of, hanging on the wall in that frame? Someone she had seen somewhere before. A gray-haired woman with a scowl. Lucie closed her eyes, erasing the scene. From far off in the room came the sound of a typewriter. Clack clack clack, it went. Clack clack clack clack clack.

"Her teeth are chattering again." Someone's voice. "Last night she snapped the thermometer in two with her teeth."

"Cover her with another blanket."

"She already has two."

"They aren't enough. Try a third."

Something heavy—sand, was it? Was she being buried in sand? Was someone making her a mermaid again?—was laid across her chest, her legs. In a moment the typing stopped.

"There." That voice again. "Still, we'll have to call in someone to look at her. It could be a morbid infection."

Lucie opened her eyes. There were *two* portraits in

the frame, not one. Both with gray hair, both with scowls, both with faces she had seen before. Where?

"The whole school will have to be quarantined."

"It may be too late."

Who was saying all that?

"We should ban all visitors."

"What visitors would she have?"

"I can't understand how anyone can be so healthy one day and so ill the next."

The portraits in their frame were badly drawn, with the lines all fuzzy and the colors blurred. She closed her eyes again and the typing started up once more.

"There go her teeth again. The blankets aren't doing any good."

"Try another," and once again someone was covering her with sand, making her a bigger mermaid than before. She tried to move her legs—her tail—but she couldn't even feel where they were.

"Just look at the color of her face."

"Like clay."

"Try the broth again." Something hard was placed against her teeth and salty water ran down her chin. The sea?

A long time after, or maybe a short time, Lucie opened her eyes and there were the portraits all over again, only now first one and then the other began to move—toward each other, away; toward each other, away. And then, suddenly, horribly, they jumped right out of the frame altogether. Side by side now, they approached, drawing nearer, nearer, until they hung like lanterns above the bed. The sand. Wherever she was.

Someone screamed.

"Lucie, stop that," one face said.

"Keep *still!*" said the other. It was Mrs. Henderson, that was who. Mrs. Henderson and Miss Pimm, standing side by side and framed by the molding of the window. "You'll only bring on more chills," Miss Pimm was saying, "carrying on like that," and her eyes grew wide so that the whites showed all around.

CHAPTER FORTY-FOUR

Better

At first Lucie couldn't find her desk, or even the space where it had been. Someone had moved the desk to a corner, and other desks and tables had crowded together, like fish in a pond, to fill the hole.

She had lain in Mrs. Henderson's room, she had just learned, for three weeks. Long enough to be noticed when she stood at the door. "Goose is back," someone said, and eyes went up.

She still felt funny. Her shoes were stiff and heavy on her feet, and now and then one knee began to quiver with an energy all its own. Also, water from the fountain, when she held it in her mouth, took on a taste that somehow wasn't right—a nice taste, though, and strangely cold.

Nobody helped her move her desk, but Emily and Anna slid their own desks apart to make way.

Things had changed a little in the room since she'd been gone. Some of the leaves on the bean vines had yellowed and grown limp, and here and there among them squat pods hung, like hidden items in a puzzle picture. There'd been a new project, too. Stretched along the walls was a row of giant posters with pictures of the nighttime sky. And a whole new series of adventures, or whatever they were, had taken place among the Pendletons. All of them had been gone all summer—*"away on holiday,"* Miss Pimm read aloud, *"visiting with their dear grandmamma"*—and Frank spoke of some very great surprise that had already occurred. Also, they seemed to have acquired a cat. Maybe that had been the surprise.

The biggest change in the room, though, was that Lucie had returned. She intruded, like an accidental spill of paint, on a landscape where she no longer belonged. All day she was looked at in surprise, and twice Rose Beth said, "It looks different in here."

CHAPTER FORTY-FIVE

Straightening Up

Everyone was lying on the floor. Olive had had a spell in the kitchen, Mr. Broome had tripped on the rug in the hall, and the baby had rocked herself out of her cradle onto the drawing room rug. The real Lucie had to stand Olive up again, as the china Lucie was gone, but it was Olive who helped Mr. Broome to his feet and put the baby back where she belonged.

"I have never seen a greater mess!" Olive exclaimed. "You would think that when a family was gone for three weeks, the house they'd left behind would be easier to clean, but just look at all this clutter. I've never seen the like."

"Dreadful," Mr. Broome agreed, still smiling his half smile. His pants were smudged and his hat was nowhere to be seen.

Little by little, Olive set the house to rights. She arranged all the dishes on the tea tray and set the piano on its pencil leg again. In the kitchen, she moved the churn across the floor and reattached the stovepipe to the wall. Mr. Broome followed just a step behind, and together they stood the icebox right side up.

Upstairs, they straightened out the toilet and returned Greenheart to his cage. "Oh, Greenheart," Olive said. "Just look at where you've been. You'll get chilblains in your legs, lying on the cold floor like this," and Greenheart answered with his three clear notes.

"At least my tub is on its feet," Olive said, in the attic now. "What a shame if it had been knocked over."

"And all that dry water spilled out," Mr. Broome added.

"There's no need to be silly, Mr. Broome." She continued to call him that, even though he was her husband. Lucie had never thought up a first name for him, and it seemed too late to give him one now.

From the drawing room, Maud began to cry. "The baby!" Olive exclaimed. "She's been left all alone!" and she hurried down the stairs. "I'm coming, I'm coming, I'm *coming!*" she shouted, while Mr. Broome followed close behind. "Just a minute," he called to Maud. *Just a meenit.*

Olive tipped herself over at the toes so she could lift the baby from its cradle. "Hush," she said, rocking back and forth on her feet, as of course she had no lap.

"Hush," she tried again, although that didn't seem to help: Maud's cries grew louder and louder. "Everybody's gone away on holiday," she explained. Olive, of course, knew this was not true, but Lucie thought it was the right thing to say to a baby. "They'll all be back very soon." Olive knew this was not true either. "They've gone to the seashore to visit with their grand-mamma, and Mr. Broome and I will look after you. Won't you like that, Maud?"

Maud wouldn't.

"Hush," Olive said again, and Mr. Broome, too, tried to tell Maud to keep still. *Kip steel,* he told her.

CHAPTER FORTY-SIX

Letters

When Lucie had finally opened her eyes in Mrs. Henderson's room—opened them, that is, so that she saw what was there—she found a stack of letters and a glass of flowers on the table by her bed.

The flowers had been picked from the bean vines on her classroom window. Lucie twisted a blossom from its stem and held it to her face. It had four petals only, creamy white, with pale green veins. One, the largest, was spread out like an open fan. Two, just within it, shielded a small miracle: an inner petal curled into the exact shape of a bird. All together they became a white fairy peacock in full display. Lucie touched it with the tip of her nail, so lightly she felt nothing at all, and watched it quiver. If only it were made of glass, of paper, of plastic, of anything other than this fragile tissue that, in a day or less, would darken at the rims, wrinkle like a blister, and die.

She moved her eyes away and saw the letters in their pile.

There were seventeen in all, and only one was in an

envelope. The rest were written on loose-leaf paper and they said nearly the same thing. "Dear Lucie, I am very sorry to learn that you are ill," they began. Then they listed four things that the class was doing while she was away. They all listed the same four, except for Rose Beth, who wrote, "The hamster smells like a zoo," instead of, "We are doing star study." They signed their letters "Sincerely yours," the complimentary close Miss Pimm had put on the board.

The letter in the envelope was from Delia.

Oh, Lucie, it began. Not "Dear" or anything. Just "Oh."

The most terrible thing ever has happened. I don't know how to begin to tell you. I'm in this horrible, horrible place, and I don't even know where it is. I've been abducted! By a bunch of awful people, I don't know who. Not only that. Everybody in the whole family, almost, was abducted, even my mother and father. Lizzie got left behind with Francy and Mr. Huggins, but she's the only one. I can't even tell you what happened, because I don't know. We were playing games in the sitting room is what I can remember, and then there was this big sort of rumpus and some people burst into the house, and they dragged us out and here I am.

It's like I'm a prisoner, but worse, because I don't know where I am. I'm not even sure if it's a house I'm in or a flat. Sometimes I'm left alone for hours in a room that has no light. Lucie, you can't imagine what it's like. There's a bed that I can't breathe in when I'm in it, it's so stuffy. And then when they come to get me—these awful people who brought me here—they make me play games that I hate. The odd thing is they think they're being nice. They call me funny names and they dress me by the hour in crazy clothes. Sometimes I go all stiff so they can't get them on, but then they yank up my arms until I shriek.

Oh, Lucie, do you think there is something you could do to help me? Do you? I can't think what it must be like for Philip, wherever he is. He's afraid of all sorts of things. He'll imagine there are goblins in his pillow. Could your mother or your father do something to find us? Ask. Tell them that I'm in this place where there's no window in my room and a bed that is like a ton of mattresses. Tell them to look for Philip, too. Also, for my mother and father. You know what they look like from the picture I sent.

Please write me straight away.

Your very best friend who needs you more than ever,
Delia

CHAPTER FORTY-SEVEN

Constellations

Miss Pimm stopped the lesson when Lucie walked through the door, and everybody looked up. It was like walking unexpectedly onto a stage.

"Where were you all afternoon, Lucie?" Miss Pimm demanded.

"I fell asleep in the library, Miss Pimm."

"No, she didn't, Miss Pimm," Charlotte said. "I was in the library and she wasn't there."

"After that I fell asleep in the Visitors' Room, Miss Pimm. Because I've been sick."

"You've been back in class for a week now, Lucie. You are recovered from your illness. Look at the clock."

Lucie did as she was told.

The clock was old and the hours were marked in X's, V's, and I's. Four I's in a row made a little picket fence where the number four should have been, and the V's and I's for the five, six and seven were upside down. Lucie had never noticed any of that before.

"What does the clock say?" Miss Pimm asked.

What would Emmett have answered to that? *It says*

nothing at all, most likely. *It doesn't have a mouth,* and he would have fallen on the floor, pleased with what he'd said. *It's got hands on its face instead,* he would have continued, and then he would have thought of something else, until Olive or somebody made him stop.

What would Olive have said to Miss Pimm, come to think of it? *Half past on the dot,* is what, and Mumma would have agreed: *Yes it is. Half past on the dot. Time for tea.* Or for beggar-my-neighbor or for donkey or for talking about school. Whatever.

"I can't hear you, Lucie."

"It's quarter to three, Miss Pimm."

"And you've been gone since noon. You are driving all of us here at Norwood Hall frantic, Lucie. Take your seat."

"Yes, Miss Pimm." *Where should I take it?* Emmett would have said.

"You are hopelessly behind as it is," Miss Pimm continued. "You missed three weeks of decimals when you were ill and two full chapters of star study."

Star study was what they were doing now. An arrangement of dots was drawn on the board, and Miss Pimm was connecting them with lines of chalk to make a triangle and an upside-down five. "This is Leo," she explained, and Rose Beth laughed. "Why is that amusing, Rose Beth?"

"Because it's funny to give a boy's name to a design?"

Rose Beth asked, trying to give a correct answer. She was dropping little bits of something through the hole that had once held an inkwell in her desk.

"Leo is a lion," Miss Pimm told her, told the class, and this time it was Emily who laughed. Miss Pimm pointed to a poster where the same arrangement of stars was surrounded by a large drawing of a lion with heavy muscles and a wild head. With a tail, even, although there were no stars to give it shape, and with teeth, too. How did anybody see a lion in a bunch of dots like that?

"With a little imagination, we can see the same creatures that the Greeks and Romans found in their heavens." Miss Pimm pointed to a horseshoe of dots that was supposed to be a set of twins. An artist had drawn their figures—with curly hair and full-lipped smiles and towels folded at their waists—around the dots. One twin held a little harp and the other a baseball bat, or maybe it was something else. Each had an arm around the other's neck, but one looked to the right and the other to the left, as though they were crossing a street. "Who can tell us the name of the twins?" Miss Pimm asked.

"Jack and Jill?" Anna tried.

The sky was darkening outside the train window and the lights went on overhead. When Lucie looked out,

she saw her own family—her mother and father together, her own self facing them—just the other side
of the train wall, riding along on a set of cushioned
seats all their own.

"There's the Great Bear." Her mother's face rested
against the window glass now, attaching itself, forehead to forehead, to its reflected twin outside.

"Where?" Lucie pressed her own face against the
pane, walling in the dark with her hands. Instantly,
the companion family disappeared and in its place distant mounds took shape, and stars hung about in the
sky. Off to the right, a sliver of moon, like a rocker
set adrift from its chair, followed at the speed of the
train. "What bear?"

"Up there, in the stars, Lucie. Can't you see? There
is its tail." With a fingernail against the window, Lucie's
mother tapped the pattern of three stars in a row. "And
there are its paws." Double tap, double tap, double
tap.

"Where?" Lucie repeated, squinting now.

"You can't see it just like that," her father told her.
"You need a pencil to connect the dots. That's what
the night sky is, Lucie. A giant dot-to-dot game. Except
they forgot to put in the numbers."

He then set about making up a dot-to-dot picture
of his own, handing her a page filled with points and
tiny numerals, one to seventy-eight. "What's it going

to be?" she asked. "I've no idea," he replied, and he leaned forward as her pencil progressed from dot to dot, like a train making stops along its way. "A cauliflower, do you think? An ice cube? London?"

"Don't tell," she said, and she covered with one hand the portion already done, so as not to guess too soon what the design would finally be. "I want it to be a surprise."

In the end, though, she never found out. She never got past number twenty-three.

CHAPTER FORTY-EIGHT

The Babbidges' Holiday

"There's been a letter from the Babbidges." Olive held a slip of paper between her hands.

"Read it aloud," Mr. Broome told her.

"*Dear Mr. and Mrs. Broome,* it says. I'm glad they finally got that right. *And Maud, We are having such a lovely time here at the seaside that we have decided to stay an extra week at least. I hope you won't mind. Lucie and Emmett are all nice and pink from the sun, and Mr. Babbidge and I are looking quite well, too. It seems a shame to return home now when it is so pleasant here, and when it's been so nasty at home. I hear there's been rain ever since we left.* How did she ever hear that?" Olive wondered.

"I wrote it in a letter," Mr. Broome explained.

"But it hasn't been raining here at all."

"I didn't say it was raining here. I said it was raining. I didn't say where."

"I think that was very foolish, Mr. Broome, especially as now they will be staying away for an extra week."

"But it is nice living here in such a quiet house. And besides, they are having a lovely time."

"Yes, they are," and Olive continued with the letter. *"We make sandpies every day, and Mr. Babbidge buries Lucie's legs to make a mermaid tail."* Olive turned to Mr. Broome. "That is not sensible. How will she ever be able to walk?"

"Maybe he made two tails—one for each leg."

Olive had no reply to that, and even if she had, she wouldn't have had a chance to make it, because Maud suddenly began to cry from her cradle in the drawing room.

"She wants feeding," Olive said, hopping quickly from the kitchen. "Here, Maud." She lifted the baby into her pipe-cleaner arms and held a speck of cookie to its mouth. To what had been its mouth: The little red dot was still smudged. "Here's some lovely tea." But it wasn't feeding that Maud wanted.

"Maybe she would like a bit of music," Mr. Broome suggested. *Beet* of music. "I'll play her a chaconne on the piano." He hopped across the room and swept his hands up and down the keyboard, while Olive danced here and there with Maud in her arms and Maud cried. "Play louder," Olive said, "so she can hear." Mr. Broome did exactly that, but Maud's cries grew louder still, until they could no longer be called cries at all. "Stop all that *screaming*," Olive commanded, but Maud paid her no attention at all.

"She misses her family, is what," Olive finally sighed.

"They're going to come back, Maud," she whispered to the side of Maud's smooth head. "They're only at the seashore, and they'll be back in a week. Two at the most. Maybe three. Look, your mumma wrote a little message to you in her letter." She lifted up the scrap of paper once again and pressed it between her hands. *"Don't forget us, little Maud, it says. We'll be home very soon. All of us—Dada and Lucie and Emmett and me. Meanwhile, here is a kiss for your cheek.* There, now," Olive went on. "See? They'll all be home quite soon, so stop that noise. *Stop it!"*

But it wasn't Maud's screams that filled the storeroom now. It was somebody else's, and they came not from the dollhouse but from the corridors upstairs.

"Somebody's ripped up our room!" The voice was Claire's. Lucie could tell, even from so far away, because of the hiccup that was almost there.

CHAPTER FORTY-NINE

Chaos

After that, it was hard to tell whose voice was whose. Two people screamed, "What happened to my bed?" at exactly the same moment, and then somebody else just screamed without saying any words at all. Pretty soon, everyone was running down the hall, yelling for Miss Pimm, for Mrs. Henderson, for anybody.

"Somebody's broken into our room, Miss Pimm!"

"Everything's upside down!"

"There's clothes and sheets thrown all over the floor."

"There's nothing left in the lockers."

"There's drawers piled all over the beds."

"There's this heap of shoes."

Finally, Miss Pimm's voice rose above the others. "Be still, all of you! Nothing will be settled by useless noise," and she marched them all back to their dormitory room.

There was silence after that, but not for long. "I know who did it!" Emily cried. "It was the *lunatic!*"

There were some gasps, and then came Daisy's voice.
"No, it wasn't. It was Goose. That's where she was all
afternoon." And there, suddenly, she was. In the doorway.

CHAPTER FIFTY

Miss Pimm's Sitting Room

"Your conduct has altered drastically, Lucie. I cannot understand it."

"Yes, Miss Pimm. No."

"You have always displayed unusual behavior, Lucie, but never until now has it taken a violent turn. I find that profoundly disturbing."

"Yes, Miss Pimm."

"I can't help wondering if perhaps your illness affected your brain. You had an unusually high fever, you know."

"Yes, Miss Pimm," Lucie answered, although she hadn't known that at all. *How* unusually high?

"It was fortunate that we called the doctor when we did."

Doctor?

"If it hadn't been for her extraordinary efforts, you would probably not be here at all."

"Here" was a room Lucie had never before seen at Norwood Hall. It was Miss Pimm's own sitting room. That's what she called it, her sitting room. "I will see you in my sitting room," she had told Lucie, although sitting was not what it was mostly meant for, as there were no chairs. It was Miss Pimm's lying-down room, maybe, or her *staying* room. This was where she stayed, when the day was over and the girls in her class came under Mrs. Henderson's care, not hers.

Right now she was sitting on the edge of what must have been her bed—an oblong platform covered with black wool. Lucie sat opposite, on the corner of a table with a lamp in its center. But of course "here" didn't mean Miss Pimm's room at all. It meant alive. "It was a close call," Miss Pimm added, and Lucie tried to imagine an answer that Emmett might have made to that.

"Yes, Miss Pimm."

"I have been connected with Norwood Hall for a good many years, Lucie, and I have never before witnessed such a scene of willful vandalism." Miss Pimm wore at her throat a carving of a woman in a shawl, pale as the inside of a shell. It *was* the inside of a shell. Miss Pimm had told the class about it one day. "This is a cameo," she had said, "and it was carved by a fine craftsman many years ago from layers of shell and stone."

She passed it around the room then, and it traveled from palm to palm like a hidden button in a game. How did people make those things, anyway, all carved like that, with a nostril you could see and a shawl that hung in folds, just like real? Lucie had pricked her finger on its pin when she'd held it in her hand, and a little smudge of blood had reddened the lady's curls. She looked now to see if the blood was still there, but the hair was the color of a peach barely ripe.

What a tiny, perfect profile the lady had, with a nose that came straight down, without a dent, from the forehead, and a jawline you could see when you moved your head. The best part was the lips: turned down at the corner, but smiling, just the same. Could she do that, she wondered, turn down her lips and make them smile at the same time?

"Stop making unsightly faces when I speak to you, Lucie. Girls with plain looks should make an effort to improve their appearance, not worsen it."

"Yes, Miss Pimm."

"Your behavior yesterday was a shock to us all. I cannot account for it. I have called you in here to tell you that we would like you to be examined by a doctor once again."

The face on the woman in the shell-pale shawl became a sudden blur.

"A doctor?"

"She can tell if you are suffering from some disorder of the brain."

"My brain is the same as ever, Miss Pimm."

216

"Then how do you explain your shocking behavior yesterday?"

"I was looking for something!"

"Looking for something! *Looking* for something? I never. I never in all my *life*. Is that the way you look for something? By ransacking an entire room? By turning beds upside down and emptying drawers on the floor? By strewing clothes and bed sheets from one wall to the other? By throwing shoes?"

"It was important, what I was looking for."

"When personal property is lost, Lucie, it is the custom at Norwood Hall to put a notice up on the Lost Property board. We then wait for the item to turn up, which it invariably does. What was it that you were looking for?"

"I don't know, Miss Pimm."

"Pick your head up. I can't hear when you speak into your collar. What is it that you lost?"

"Personal property, Miss Pimm."

CHAPTER FIFTY-ONE

Mrs. Babbidge's Letter

"There's been another letter from the Babbidges," Olive announced. A new strip of paper was pressed between her hands and she bent forward to study it. *"Dear one and all,* it begins."

"Which is the one and which is the all, I wonder?" Mr. Broome interrupted.

Olive thought for a while. "Maud must be the one, and we must be the all," she finally said.

"But there are only two of us. Two is not all. Two is both. She should have said 'Dear one and both.'"

"So she should," Olive agreed. She held the paper up to her face once again. "Oh, dear," she exclaimed, reading to herself. "You will never guess what has happened. Both Lucie and Emmett have come down with chicken pox!"

"Come down with them? Come down where? The staircase?"

"Mr. Broome, they both *have* chicken pox, and that is a very dreadful thing."

"Well, they should have left them upstairs to begin with."

"Listen to what she says, Mr. Broome," and Olive began to read aloud. *"Lucie and Emmett have both come down with chicken pox. They look quite wretched, poor things. We don't want Maud to get sick, too, and so we will have to remain here until they recover. I can't say how much longer that will be. Weeks, maybe.* Oh, Mr. Broome, how very terrible that is."

"Terrible," Mr. Broome agreed. "What is it that they are going to recover?"

"She doesn't say."

"A chair, most likely. Most people recover chairs, when the arms get worn, but sofas, too, sometimes."

"Mr. Broome! You are being as ridiculous as Emmett," and that seemed true. Now that Emmett was gone, Lucie made up silly things for Mr. Broome to say instead.

Olive put her face up to the letter once again, but just at that moment Maud began to screech from her cradle. Now that she was older, she no longer mewed when she was unhappy, but let out long, painful yells.

"Oh, Mr. Broome, what shall we tell her?" Olive cried, hopping into the drawing room. "She thinks her family is coming back soon, and now they are staying away goodness knows how long. Just listen to her cry,

Mr. Broome. See if you can make her stop."

"I will, as soon as she is quiet," he answered, sounding more like Emmett than ever. "There's no use talking to her if she can't hear."

"That makes no sense." And Olive lifted Maud from her cradle.

"Maud," she said. "Do listen. Your mumma and your dada miss you very, very much, and they each send you a kiss. Here it is." Olive's face clicked against the baby's smooth head, once, twice. "They want to come back to see you, but they can't just yet, because Lucie and Emmett are sick. But as soon as they are well, they will all come back together. Won't that be nice?"

But Mr. Broome was right. There was no use talking to Maud when she was screaming so loud, and Olive soon gave up. Instead, she walked from room to room with Maud in her arms, and when that didn't work, she slid her down the stair rail into Mr. Broome's hands. "Do you like that, Maud?" she asked. "It's a very special ride, just for you."

Either Maud liked it a great deal or the breath was knocked out of her. In any case, she stopped crying. Olive slid her up the stair rail after that, and then down again, over and over, while Mr. Broome stood at the bottom with his arms straight out. "This is a very fine thing to do," he observed. "It keeps the baby quiet and it polishes the banister at the same time."

"That's not kind, Mr. Broome," Olive told him. "We are keeping Maud happy so she won't miss her family, and see how happy she is. She hasn't cried in over ten minutes."

"That's because she's asleep," Mr. Broome pointed out, and sure enough, she was. Olive carried her into the drawing room and returned her to her cradle.

"I wonder," Mr. Broome said as he and Olive tiptoed out, two feet at a time. "When chickens get sick, do they get Maud pox?"

"Stop being silly," Olive said, just as she used to when Emmett had been there.

CHAPTER FIFTY-TWO

Delia's Letter

Two strange things have happened. (No "Dear" or "Oh," this time.) One is good and the other is terrible. The good thing is that I am together once again with my mother and father and with Philip. They arrived suddenly last night with no explanation. One minute they weren't there and the next minute they were. Most things happen that way, don't you think? One minute they haven't happened, and the next minute they have and everything is different forever.

We're not back in our house, though, and that's the terrible thing. We all got transported—I can't even say how—to some dreadful dark room. A chamber is what, like they used to have in the Middle Ages. It's piled to the ceiling with I don't know what, and there are no windows in the walls at all. Just a large round hole in the roof. It makes a circle of light on the floor, and we take turns standing in it. When it's my turn, I write letters to you. When it's Philip's turn, he stands with an open box he found, collecting the light beams, he says, so he can use them when he's back in the dark. He's as stupid as ever, but at least he's here.

Every day some awful person comes and bounces us around.

She talks as though we're babies—my mother and my father, too—and she pulls our clothing on and off for no reason I can see.

Mostly what I do is think about what's happening outside while I'm in here. I keep thinking, what if it's a special day out there that will never come again, and it's all going on without me? Do you think days happen when you're not there to see them? I sometimes wonder. I always like to be there when it's a special day, like on the first day of summer. I stand outside on that day from daybreak until dark, watching and watching, because that's the longest day of the year, and I don't want to miss any of it. That way, I don't feel half sad when there's less and less day after that.

Here's something I want: You know those days where the numbers in the date are all the same, like 3/3/33 and 4/4/44, all the way up to 9/9/99? Well, I want to be alive for all of those days, so I can celebrate them all day long. Here's how: First, I'll write out the date all over the pavement, and on fences and walls, and in the underground, and on buses, and in the sky with one of those planes that make smoke. Then I'll put it on a sign on a stick and run up and down all the streets where everyone can see, and in the park, too, and down by the sea. I'll scratch the date in the sand by the sea, all over, until there is no space left on the whole beach, and by then the whole day will be over and I'll be happy. That's what I want to do, and I hope and pray that I'm not still here in this chamber or whatever it is, when the next one of those days comes by.

The only good thing about the person who's in charge here is she posts my letters. I'm sure she reads what I say, but I don't care. This is for her: I think you are horrid.

Lots of love from your best friend,
Delia

CHAPTER FIFTY-THREE

The Spelling Bee

Lucie had already been ordered to sit down. The only other girl at her seat so far was Emily, but then the spelling bee had only just begun. Emily, in fact, had spelled her word correctly, but she'd forgotten to pronounce it aloud before and after it was spelled. Those were the rules. "Pronounce your word in a good strong voice," Miss Pimm had told them, "both before you spell it and when you are through," but Emily hadn't remembered until it was too late.

"It is not enough just to know how to spell a word correctly," Miss Pimm said. "You must listen to directions as well," and Emily said "Yes, Miss Pimm." "A spelling bee is like driving a car," Miss Pimm went on, "where knowing the rules is as important as having mechanical skill," but it wasn't like driving a car. It was like a game of giant steps, where you could do everything right but get punished just the same. Sometimes Lucie would watch Daisy or Enid twirl across the length of the Grounds, being an umbrella or a dancing doll, only to be ordered back to the starting line for not having said, "May I?"

Lucie hadn't pronounced her word, but then she hadn't spelled it out either. When Miss Pimm had said, "Dismay," Lucie had answered, "Dismay?" and Miss Pimm had told her to sit down. "Write your word twenty times and study it until you have learned it by heart." Emily had to write her word twenty times, too, although she'd learned it long before.

The point of Lucie's pencil snapped in two, leaving a jagged hole and making her stomach strangely drop.

"Where are you going, Lucie?"

"To sharpen my pencil, Miss Pimm."

And now she had a palmful of curly pencil gratings, the color of a brick, but with edges that stained her fingers silver black. One by one she rolled her fingertips on the paper to make smudges. Five silver smudges in a row there were, each in the shape of a head. Five of them, like a family: The thumb was the baby, the pinky was the little brother, and the rest were the mother and the father and the big sister. She gave them all faces, arms, and legs, and, for the baby, a bonnet full of frills.

"What are you doing, Lucie?"

"Writing my spelling word, Miss Pimm." With a swing of her pencil, she connected all their arms, hand to hand, to make a chain. Then she smoothed them all out, darkening the edge of her hand.

"No, she's not, Miss Pimm." Anna had misspelled her word and was sitting now at her desk. "She's making pictures."

"Put that away this minute," and Lucie snapped them shut in the dark of her desk.

When the train shot into the tunnel, all the lights went out without reason, or so it seemed. Maybe the lights had gone out first, matching the inside of the train to the dark of the night, and *then* there'd been the tunnel. Maybe there'd been no tunnel at all. Just dark, inside and out. But the stars had disappeared, too, and so had the thin yellow rocker of a moon. So there must have been a tunnel—or a wall, at least. Something. One minute, there had been a whole world out there. The next it had all, like the peep show at the beach, gone black.

And the noise. When had that begun? When the lights went out, or just before? Lucie had heard it through her arms and her legs before she felt it in her ears. It made a rattle in her knees, and her elbows boomed like gongs. Even in that moment when everything was still—when the first noise had stopped and the screams had not begun—she could feel that steady clangor in her bones.

The last sound she heard was her very own voice. "What was that?" she had whispered, or maybe screamed, but of course she had gotten no reply.

Lucie peered through the inkwell hole in her desk. Three of the silver black fingerprint heads lay in the center of the pale disk of light. The father, the mother, and the big sister, they were, all together. She stared at them a long time, keeping the three heads in focus within their round frame, and then she brought her eye closer and closer until it covered the hole completely and the three heads vanished in the dark.

"Pick your head up, Lucie. This is not the time or the place to take a nap." *Pick your head up.* What would Emmett have answered to that? What silly, fresh, sassy, wonderful thing would he have said to Miss Pimm?

"Did you hear me, Lucie?"

"Yes, Miss Pimm." What would he have *said*?

Charlotte and Jane were standing side by side against the wall. "Restaurant," Miss Pimm said, and she let Charlotte get all the way through the word before telling her it was wrong.

Jane was the winner of the spelling bee, and she got to crayon her nails green while the others all wrote out their misspelled words twenty times on a sheet of lined paper.

"Where is your word practice, Lucie?"

"In my desk, Miss Pimm," Lucie answered. Now she could see all five fingerprint heads, one beside the other in a row. She leaned forward and blew a word through the hole: "Hello," she blew, and she waited for its message to travel, like an electric buzz, from the baby's open hand to her sister's, to her father's, to her mother's, to her brother's at the other side of the page.

"Hello," she said again, and then—suddenly, amazingly—she knew where to look for the dolls.

CHAPTER FIFTY-FOUR

"Good-bye"

The mother doll was the one that needed the most straightening up. Her dress must have been taken off and put on again a hundred times. A rip appeared where the sleeve was attached, and the lace that edged the hem hung loose in the back, as though she'd caught it in her heel.

The other dolls didn't look too bad, all in all. The girl doll's dress needed smoothing all around, and the sash was gone, but her face was the same and her arms and legs still swung back and forth. The boy doll's shirt had a new spot in front, but it rubbed right away with Lucie's spit. The father doll had lost his hat, and his shoes were badly scuffed, but he looked just as handsome as ever. And, of course, the clothespin dolls and Maud had been safely left behind, so nothing needed doing to fix them up.

The best place for the mother doll, Lucie decided, was the sofa, so that was where she seated her—in the corner, leaving room for someone else. The baby in its cradle should go at her feet, just as before, and the father doll should be stood inside the door, as though he'd just that moment come home.

The clothespin maid would probably best be leaned against the icebox, where she wouldn't fall down, and the doll who was her husband could go—where? Beside the table in the kitchen would be good. He could be talking to the maid doll, or maybe he could be going to sleep standing up, or he could be listening to the sound of some far-off music with his eyes closed. Any one of those.

The boy doll was best put in his room, seated on the floor beside his Noah's ark. The animals needed lining up, and that took rather a long time, as some of them had only three legs. An elephant and a camel, in the end, were given naps.

And what of the girl doll? She could be seated on the piano bench, ready to play a chaconne for the family, with the bird in its cage at her side. Or she could be placed on the sofa, with the mother doll's arm resting on her shoulder, as though they were telling each other things. That was probably best, and that is where she was put.

There, Lucie thought. All nice and neat. Everything just as it should be. No, not quite everything. The piano leg needed to be straightened. But that took just a moment, and all that needed doing now was covering the house with the sweater. "Good-bye," she said, as she did so. "Good-bye," she said. Out loud, this time; not in her head.

"Good-bye." How long, she wondered, would it take? How long now before Delia and her family were rescued and restored to their house? How long for everything to stop being strange? For odd words to stop appearing in Delia's mouth? For Francy to stop tripping? For the piano keys to stop brightening by themselves?

One week? Two? Would it happen right away? At this very moment, were Delia and her family sitting all together, looking happily at one another and sighing and saying, "Well, thank goodness that's all over" or however they said things like that in England? Were they? Was Delia's mother right now asking, "But how did such odd things happen to us?" And was Delia wondering that, too?

Maybe. Maybe Delia right this minute was wondering aloud why everything had been so strange in their house for so long and then, suddenly, wasn't strange at all. Nobody would be able to provide an answer, but Delia very soon would find out. Lucie herself would tell her.

In a letter.

She had reached the storeroom door when she heard a tiny crash behind her. The sweater had to be removed then, so she could reach inside and stand the maid doll up once again, very carefully this time. She even held her open hand above the maid doll's head for a while, as though to steady the air around it. "Good-bye," she said aloud once more, and she draped the sweater over the roof, letting the sleeves trail along the floor like two broad paths.

CHAPTER FIFTY-FIVE

Stolen

"Hey, somebody took my dolls!" With one hand, Rose Beth propped her desk lid up. With the other, she churned up all the papers inside. "Yesterday they were right *here*! And now they're *gone*!"

"Rose Beth, you are interrupting a lesson."

"Yes, Miss Pimm. But somebody took my dolls. I had them right here in my desk."

"What dolls? Where did you get dolls?"

"Nowhere, Miss Pimm. I found them."

"They were the lunatic's," Emily said.

"Yes, but after that they were lots of ours," Claire added. "Mine was the lady one."

"And the girl one was mine," Daisy said. "I kept it in my drawer, in a tissue box for a bed."

"But then I traded stuff for all of them," Rose Beth interrupted, "and they were mine. I kept them in my desk and now they're *gone*."

"Before that they were the lunatic's," Emily reminded Miss Pimm.

"I thought I made it very clear, Rose Beth, that playthings were not allowed in the classroom." A crescent of white was beginning to show at the lower rims of Miss Pimm's eyes.

"Yes, Miss Pimm. They weren't playthings. They were these four dolls, with clothes and all. They looked like real people almost, except smaller, and somebody took them."

"Nobody can take things from this room while I am in it."

"After, then. When school was over. At night, probably."

"The room is locked at night, Rose Beth."

"Well, then, somebody came in through the window, Miss Pimm. They came in at night and took all the dolls out of my desk."

"You are wasting class time, Rose Beth. You should learn to look after your things and keep them where they belong."

"Yes, Miss Pimm, but they belonged in my desk."

"It was the lunatic, I bet," Emily said.

CHAPTER FIFTY-SIX

Rescued

Dear Lucie,

You will never guess what has happened! We got rescued! Somebody came and swept us all up helter-skelter and delivered us home. None of us can remember quite how it came about. My father thinks he rescued us, but he is wrong. I saw somebody strange come through the door, I know I did. And my mother says she saw a skinny hand. Philip says it was a kangaroo, with a pocket that had buttons, but he got that from a comic he read.

Anyway, yesterday was our first day home. It was a lovely day. I just stood still in the middle of it, not moving and not moving and not moving, so it would last and last.

We were all a bit untidy when we arrived. You could see my mother's elbow through a hole in her sleeve, and Philip's shirt was stained with something blue. Ink, I think. My father's hair stood up in bits and pieces and his clothes looked like those maps where the mountains are all bumps. Also, his hat was missing. Francy said we looked a fright, but she would have said that no matter what.

I don't think Mr. Huggins was too glad to see us back. "I

liked the peace and quiet," he kept saying. "But there is peace and quiet now we're here," my mother told him, and there is. Everything is back the way it was. And not the way it was before we all were hidden away. Before that. Before everything started going queer. Of course, we have Lizzie now, and Francy's married to Mr. Huggins, so it's not exactly the same, but there are no more earthquakes and Francy's stopped tripping on the cat all the time. Also, Philip doesn't say his stupid things anymore.

I thought maybe when I got home there'd be a letter from you, but there wasn't.

Lots of love,
Delia

237

CHAPTER FIFTY-SEVEN

The Second Miracle

Today's botany lesson was on the life cycle of the bean. The beans that everyone had planted two, three, months ago had reached the end of their life cycle. The leaves that just a week before had filled the windowpanes with green were shriveled into little scraps, thin as tissue paper, yellow as sand. The vines themselves had loosened from their cords and were hanging, limp as threads, along the sill.

Everything had turned ugly. The pale peacock flowers of last month had been transformed—like fairy princesses into toads—and now were stiff green pods, fat with lumps. The spiderwebs were gone, and the fragile green curls to which they'd clung were brittle, and sharp as broken fingernails.

Miss Pimm stood at one end of the window wall. "The second miracle of which I spoke is about to be revealed. Who can recall the first miracle of the beans?"

"They turned into a jungle," Enid said.

"They sprouted and produced a multitude of vines," Miss Pimm said. "The bean plants, class, are now mature. Who can tell us the meaning of the word 'mature'?"

"It means not acting like a baby or whining all the time," Jane said.

"It means being quiet in assembly," Anna added.

"It means you're old," Daisy said.

"A mature plant is one that has reached the end of its productive life," Miss Pimm told them. "It has completed its natural growth. Portions of it have withered and died. What portions? Claire?"

"The brown ones, Miss Pimm."

"The support system is one portion of the plant that has died, class. What is the support system of the plant? Lucie?"

Lucie ran her hand across the ruled paper on her desk as though she were clearing it of crumbs, and in the upper corner, as Miss Pimm had taught them, she set down her address—Norwood Hall—and the date.

"Lucie?"

"I don't know, Miss Pimm."

"Jane?"

"The strings and everything, Miss Pimm, that it climbs on. And the cord from the window shade."

"The *vines* are the support system, class. They support the fruit and the food manufacturers. Who can tell us what part of the plant manufactures food?"

Nobody could.

"The *leaves* manufacture food for the plant. They, too, have died. The plant no longer requires food. And what part of the plant is the fruit? Lucie?"

Lucie had just finished the salutation. "The 'salutation' is a greeting," Miss Pimm had said. "It is your way of greeting your correspondent. Follow your salutation with a comma if your letter is to a friend, with a colon if it is to an adult you don't know." Lucie picked a comma.

"Look at me, Lucie."

"Yes, Miss Pimm."

"What portion of the plant is the fruit?"

"I don't know, Miss Pimm."

"Daisy?"

"Fruit, Miss Pimm? You mean like apples?"

Miss Pimm held up, by the stub of its tail, a long green pod. "The fruit is that portion of the plant that bears seeds when ripe." The lumps inside bulged through its skin like sourballs hidden in a cheek. "This pod is a ripened fruit," and she ran a thumbnail along a seam at its side. In an instant five white beans burst into her palm. "These are the second miracle." She paused a long, long moment, and repeated, "The second miracle."

Then she walked up and down the aisles so each girl could see the second miracle for herself. "Each of you, two months ago, planted a bean just like one of these," she said. "From each of your beans there came a plant that grew and grew into a sturdy vine. That was the first miracle. And as it grew, it prepared a wonderful gift. These new beans are its gift. That is the second miracle. Although the plant itself has died, it has left behind dozens and dozens of beans from which new plants can grow. And each of those will produce dozens of beans of its own."

She had reached the end of the aisle by now, and she let Charlotte inspect the miracles crowding one another in her hand. "Each and every bean holds the promise of its own immortality. The cycle of life continues forever. Repeat that, Charlotte."

" 'The cycle of life continues forever.' Look, Miss Pimm, the beans are the jumping kind. I just saw one wiggle," and both Claire and Rose Beth twisted around in their seats to see.

Miss Pimm proceeded along the aisles, holding out her hand to each girl. "Life renews itself," she told them. "Say that after me, Lucie."

The main part of a letter was what Miss Pimm called the body. "The body can be long or short," she had told them, making Claire laugh. The body of Lucie's letter wasn't either one—just three quarters of a page, so far—but then she wasn't finished quite yet.

"Say that after me, Lucie."

"I didn't hear, Miss Pimm."

"Rose Beth, repeat what I just said."

" 'Life renews itself,' Miss Pimm. Can we plant the new beans all over again? Can we keep on planting them again and again until the vines fill up the whole room?"

"The whole *school*," Anna said.

"The world," said Enid, but Miss Pimm said there would be no more bean planting at all, as they were finished with botany for the year.

She turned up a new aisle. "From death there is birth," she announced. "Always remember that, class. From death there is birth. What is it that I just said, Lucie?"

The body of Lucie's letter now took up three whole pages, and it was time at last for what Miss Pimm called the complimentary close. "The 'complimentary close' is the letter writer's way of saying good-bye," she had taught them. "If your letter is a formal one, your close will be 'Yours truly' or 'Very truly yours.' If it is a less formal letter, you will close it with 'Sincerely.' "

Lucie didn't pick any of those. She wrote "Love." "Love, Lucie."

"What is it that I just said, Lucie?"

"I don't know, Miss Pimm." She put a nice big loop in the *L* of Love and another in the *L* of her name. Then, as an afterthought, she drew in each loop a little face: an eye, an eye, a mouth—dot, dot, circle.

"What is it you are doing, Lucie?"

"Nothing, Miss Pimm," which by now was true. Her pen lay in its canoe-shaped groove at the top edge of her desk.

"She's writing, Miss Pimm," Anna said.

"What are you writing, Lucie?"

"Nothing, Miss Pimm." She turned the pages over and spread her fingers wide across them.

"It's a letter, Miss Pimm," Anna said. "It's to her personage. I already saw. And it said a lot of things you're not supposed to say to personages. It said all about herself and everything. Not about her career. It said about school. It said about you."

"We do not write letters during lessons, Lucie. Repeat what I just said."

"We do not write letters during lessons, Miss Pimm."

"Look at me when you speak."

"Yes, Miss Pimm."

"And pick your head up."

For a long, long moment, Lucie didn't answer or even move. Then, suddenly, she stood up straight and tall and, with her eyes on Miss Pimm, spoke in a voice both strong and clear. "How can I, Miss Pimm?" she said, at last saying aloud what had before been spoken only in her head. "How can I, when it never fell off in the first place?" and Rose Beth, Daisy, and Anna, from different corners of the room, stopped what they were doing and looked up at her in surprise.

ABOUT THE AUTHOR

Sylvia Cassedy is the author of several books for
children, including BEHIND THE ATTIC WALL,
which was a 1983 ALA Notable Children's
Book, a 1983 *SLJ* Best Book of the Year, and
an IRA/CBC Children's Choice for 1984; and
M. E. AND MORTON, a 1987 ALA Notable Children's Book, a 1987 *SLJ* Best Book of the Year,
as well as a 1987 ALA *Booklist* Childrens' Editors'
Choice.

A longtime teacher of creative writing, Ms.
Cassedy was graduated from Brooklyn College
in New York and studied in the Department of
Writing Seminars at The Johns Hopkins Uni-
versity in Baltimore.